Wicked Night Games . . . A H...
Untamed . . . Unmasked . . . Taboo

The sensual, seductive novels of
KATHLEEN LAWLESS
are erotically charged adventures sure to leave you satisfied . . .
. . . and reviewers can't get enough, either!

"THE SEX IS RIVETING. . . . The story is fresh. . . . The dialogue is snappy and unique." —*Romance Junkies*

"A WONDERFUL, HEATED TALE." —*The Best Reviews*

"HIGHLY ENTERTAINING. . . . Imagine Nancy Drew meets *Sex and the City*!" —*Roundtable Reviews*

"DO NOT MISS THIS BOOK. . . . Lawless weaves romance, intrigue, and excitement into an impressive tapestry." —*Romance Reviews Today*

"A highly erotic page-turner." —*Fallen Angel Reviews*

"An amusing, spirited, adventurous tale." —*Romantic Times*

"An engaging erotic romance." —*Midwest Book Review*

XXX
Marks the Spot

Kathleen Lawless

POCKET BOOKS
New York   London   Toronto   Sydney

Pocket Books
A Division of Simon & Schuster, Inc.
1230 Avenue of the Americas
New York, NY 10020

First Pocket Books trade paperback edition April 2008.

POCKET and colophon are registered trademarks of Simon & Schuster, Inc.

For information about special discounts for bulk purchases, please contact Simon & Schuster Special Sales at 1-800-456-6798 or business@simonandschuster.com.

Designed by Laura McBride

Manufactured in the United States of America

10 9 8 7 6 5 4 3 2 1

Library of Congress Cataloging-in-Publication Data

Lawless, Kathleen.
    XXX marks the spot / Kathleen Lawless.—1st Pocket Books trade paperback 3d.
        p. cm.
    I. Title.
    PS3612.A9444X87 2008
    813'.6--dc22

ISBN-13: 978-1-4165-3274-3 (pbk.)
ISBN-10:   1-4165-3274-9 (pbk.)

Acknowledgments

Special thanks for my golf pro buddy, Bill Wakeham, for his help on and off the course.

A huge thank-you to Sheri, Brenda, and Nancy for their brainstorming at the Beach House. As well as Donna Faye, who lugged back armloads of reference info from her vacation in the deep South golf resorts, and Kate, who gave me Ted October!

And, as always, Micki Nuding, for her enthusiasm for my work and her keen editor's eye.

To all my single girlfriends who believe well-behaved women rarely make history. May we all become legends!

Justine

Sexcapades

collect:

— your date's boxers
— his favorite golf glove
— a snip of his chest hair

score:

— a shooter he slurps from your belly button
— an extravagant piece of jewelry
— a picture of his penis

enjoy:

— sex in a limo *Fun!*
— water sex (indoors or out)
— sex outdoors (double points for daytime)
— skinny-dipping with your date
— dress-up sex *Can I?*
— him as your slave, bondage included

Lisa

Sexcapades

collect:

— your date's boxers
— his favorite golf glove
— a snip of his chest hair *How on earth?*

score:

— a shooter he slurps from your belly button
— an extravagant piece of jewelry
— a picture of his penis

enjoy:

— sex in a limo
— water sex (indoors or out) *Yikes!*
— sex outdoors (double points for daytime)
— skinny-dipping with your date
— dress-up sex?
— him as your slave, bondage included *Not possible!*

Kennedy

Sexcapades

Did I make this too easy?

collect:

___ your date's boxers

___ his favorite golf glove

___ a snip of his chest hair

score:

___ a shooter he slurps from your belly button

___ an extravagant piece of jewelry

___ a picture of his penis

enjoy:

___ sex in a limo

___ water sex (indoors or out)

___ sex outdoors (double points for daytime)

___ skinny-dipping with your date

___ dress-up sex

___ him as your slave, bondage included

Chapter One

"Remember girls," Kennedy said as she led her two friends through the clubhouse to the bar, "tonight is just for practice. Our sexcapades don't officially start until tomorrow."

"Midnight or daybreak?" Justine asked.

Lisa smiled. Typical Justine-like question; her friend had voiced dozens ever since their plane landed on Walker Hook and Kennedy presented them with this irresistible challenge.

Lisa, normally the quietest of the three, was determined to show her friends that she could play as wild as they could.

"Your interpretation of tomorrow," Kennedy said as she

wangled a spot for the three of them at the bar before she scampered off.

"Gotta admire her style," Justine said as their vivacious, redheaded friend lost no time in becoming the center of attention among a group of male golfers. "When I see her like this I wonder, is she for real? Or just so deep into her public relations persona that Kennedy ceases to exist?"

"I doubt even Kennedy knows the answer to that one," Lisa said.

"I have *all* the answers." Kennedy squidged in between them and linked an arm around each of their shoulders. "Smile. The long, tall Texan's taking our picture. He's calling us the blonde, the brunette, and the redhead."

Lisa turned her attention to the man with the camera. Very yummy. "Think it's true what they say about Texas?"

"That everything's bigger? I sure hope to find out." With a quick kiss to the cheek of each of her friends, Kennedy scampered back to her waiting fans.

"You know she'll win. This is her kind of game." Lisa slipped her hand into her skirt pocket and fingered the folds of the sexcapades hunt Kennedy had distributed upon their arrival at the luxurious private villa where they were staying on the island.

"Kennedy went to a lot of trouble to surprise us with this vacation and invent an excuse to behave outrageously. And she did it because she loves us."

"I know," Lisa said. "I'm just freaking at the thought of even kissing someone new, never mind anything else. It might be easier to get my wallet out right now."

"I don't know about you." Justine ran a hand through her thick chestnut curls that Lisa, with her fine, straight blonde hair, had always envied. "But I fully intend to give Kennedy a run for her money."

"Me too," Lisa said quickly. Whoever lost paid their bar tab for the week.

How hard can it be? Lisa chided herself. *I used to be a first-class flirt. Just because I married a loser doesn't mean I've forgotten how to attract a man.*

"Time to troll. Wish me luck." She navigated her way through the room, pleased to see more than one man giving her the bar-code. *They're probably all married and looking for a quick, easy diversion.*

Stop that, she told herself. Not all men cheat.

Suddenly the meet-market atmosphere of the bar became stifling and she stepped out onto the wraparound veranda. It was blessedly quiet, and the balmy warmth felt good compared to Seattle's typical soggy spring. She breathed the tropical air, heavy with the scent of magnolias. In the background, the rhythmic chirping of the watering system did its part to keep the golf course lush and green.

"A pretty lady without a flower is a crime against nature," said a deep masculine voice from the shadows. The voice's owner stepped forward and presented her with a lily. "Please allow me to right that wrong."

Not knowing what else to do, Lisa took the flower and buried her nose in its center. "Thank you." She gave her companion a covert once-over. Nice-looking without being flashy.

Dark hair, dark eyes, a cute dimple. "Does that line usually get results?"

"I wouldn't know; I've never used it before." He was dressed in the golfer's uniform: crisply pressed pants in a tasteful neutral with a matching, discreetly logo'd golf shirt.

"I'm Rich," her companion said, extending a hand her way. Before she could offer him hers, he brushed her cheek with his fingertips. "You have pollen on your face."

"Oh." Lisa didn't know what to say or where to look. Her face was burning and it took every ounce of self-preservation not to grab his hand and hold it against her cheek.

It's natural to want to jump from one relationship to another, her counselor's words rang in her head. *But it's not smart. Take the time to explore yourself. To learn about Lisa.*

"Rich. Is that your name or a financial summary?"

His smile lit up his eyes and made him even more attractive. "Better make that Richard. I'm not used to following a beautiful but sad-looking woman to see if I can make her laugh."

Lisa stiffened. "I'm not sad. I'm on vacation."

"I was watching you earlier. You hide it well, but there's a faint shadow behind your smile."

Before she fully digested the fact that he'd been watching her, a second man stuck his head out the door. "Hey, Rich. Early tee time tomorrow. You coming?"

"Be right there." He turned to Lisa. "I hope to see you again. Maybe next time you'll tell me your name."

"It's Lisa," she called after him.

Tucking the flower behind her ear, she turned and went back inside.

Justine raised her brow at the sight of the lily. "A conquest so soon?"

"Perhaps." Lisa glanced quickly around the bar but Richard was nowhere in sight.

"I think the time change is getting to me." Justine slid off the stool and jangled the car keys. "You ready to go?"

"I guess. Where's Kennedy?"

Justine cocked her head to where Kennedy's shiny red head was tilted against her Texan. "It appears she's having a practice round. I need my beauty sleep to be in fighting form."

Outside the clubhouse, Lisa slid into the passenger seat of their rented Jag convertible. "You never said much about when you and Mr. Married split up."

Justine shrugged. "You were going through your own stuff with Les. My problems seemed petty in comparison."

"Nothing about supporting a friend is ever petty."

"Lisa, he was married. You were always pretty vocal concerning your view on men who cheat."

"Oh." Yes, she'd struggled with Les's infidelity. For some reason, it had been harder to accept than his death. She laid a hand on Justine's arm, forcing her friend to look at her. "Did you know he was married, or did he lie to you?"

Justine's lips thinned. "I knew he was married; and yes, he lied. He said they were estranged. He was leaving. They weren't sleeping together."

"None of which was true, I take it?"

"When his wife got pregnant, he didn't even have the decency to tell me. Someone else did." Her eyes were shiny as she blinked furiously. "He knew I wanted to have a baby and was just waiting for him to be free. More fool me. But I'm glad to be here."

"Me too," Lisa said. "This is going to be a whole lot of fun."

Justine started the ignition and the car's headlights came on, illuminating Kennedy as she broke out of a very tight clinch and tossed a tiny wave to her disappointed suitor before sashaying toward the car.

"What happened?" Lisa flipped the seat forward so Kennedy could climb in the back.

"Bad kisser," Kennedy said, running her fingers through her shoulder-length hair, fluffing back its bounce.

"How bad?" Justine asked.

"Let's just say I think my tonsils drowned."

"EEEEWWWW!"

"If I don't want that mouth on mine, I sure don't want it anyplace else," Kennedy said. "He used his tongue like a battering ram." She pulled out a mirror and lipstick and inspected the damage. "How about you two?"

"We're not quite as quick off the mark as you are," Justine said. "Do you think there's anything to eat at the villa?"

"We'll get Miles to make us something."

"Welcome back, darlings," Miles sang out as they tumbled into the villa, arm-in-arm.

"Oh, good. You're still up." Kennedy tossed her bag on the couch, sparing the barest glance at their surroundings. The girls had oohed and aahed when they first arrived, forcing Kennedy to take a second look—at her life, as well as her surroundings. She was accustomed to the best, along with someone who provided it. What fun to share with the others things she took for granted, like this luxury villa with a private swimming pool and live-in butler.

She *was* spoiled, but why have it any other way? Her thoughts darkened. Except for work. All those nubile twenty-somethings the agency had hired lately were making her feel old and tired, and she didn't enjoy the feeling.

"So . . ." Miles said expectantly. "I'm waiting to live vicariously through all of you, so spill. I prepared a little midnight snack."

"You're a marvel," Kennedy said. "Will you marry me?"

"Kennedy, love, not even if I preferred women over men would I marry you. You'd break my heart a million times."

"You're right," Kennedy said. "I'm not the settling down type. Much better you and I stay friends."

"There isn't much to tell." Justine pounced on the plate of bruschetta. "Kennedy picked up some guy from Texas who didn't understand that saliva is a condiment, not a main course. And some dude hit on Lisa with the 'pretty lady, pretty flower' line."

"Try the *ceviche*," Miles said. "I just made it."

"Out of this world," Lisa said.

"Is there any champagne left?" Kennedy asked.

"If there isn't, we'll open more."

Four glasses were quickly filled and raised together in a toast. "To the hunt for Ted October," the girls sang out in unison.

"And to Miles, for agreeing to keep score," Kennedy added.

"Anything for you, darling. You were my favorite of all Mr. Macho's dates."

Kennedy batted her lashes. "Shucks, I bet you say that to all the girls."

"Only the ones who are nice to me. Now tell me, why Ted October?"

"There was this hunk calendar we all had. Mr. October was the hunkiest and had signed it Ted. It kind of became a moniker for Mr. Right."

"Surely that's not how you three met," Miles said.

"No," Justine said. "Once upon a time we were all dating men who golfed, and wound up taking golf lessons together."

"The men are history," Kennedy said airily. "The friendship stuck. And here we are, once more on the hunt for the perfect man."

The chime of the doorbell interrupted their banter, and Kennedy glanced over at Miles. "Expecting a little late-night booty call?"

"I wish." Miles put down his glass and headed for the door. "More likely a tipsy neighbor at the wrong villa. They all look pretty much the same in the dark."

He returned in seconds, trailing a colorful gauzy scarf through the air with an exaggerated flourish. Behind him, a dark-haired man filled the doorway.

"Kennedy, I believe this is yours?"

"It is," she cooed, eyes locked on the yummy raven-haired specimen of manhood behind Miles as she made her way to his side. "And I believe there is a reward for its safe return."

"Your beautiful smile is more than reward enough."

Kennedy gave a theatrical sigh. "A gentleman through and through. I insist you stay and share a glass of champagne with me and my friends, Mr. . . . ?"

"Sam Watson," he said with an easy smile.

"I'm Kennedy James, and these are my two best friends, Justine and Lisa. You met Miles at the door. How did you ever track me down?"

"I just missed you in the parking lot, but managed to follow you here. I was worried about the late hour, but since the lights were still on . . ." He didn't bother finishing his sentence.

"Most resourceful." Kennedy slowly circled him as if he wore a "for sale" sign. "Where are you staying?"

"Just down the road."

"And for how long?" Visual complete, she handed him a glass of champagne, leaning in close as she did so. A girl could tell a lot by a man's choice of fragrance and this one didn't disappoint, sporting a subtle blend of citrus and woods.

"I'll be in and out a fair amount over the next short while."

Kennedy smiled a secret smile. She'd been thinking the same thing, but not in the way he meant.

"Doesn't that interfere with the golf game?"

"It might," he said, looking down at her, the hint of a smile playing with his sexy lips. "If I were here to golf."

Her hormones kicked into overdrive, eager to suggest a few rounds of her favorite recreational activity.

"So you're not here on vacation," Kennedy said with a mock pout, pretending to straighten the collar of his shirt, letting her fingertips linger near his collarbone.

"Being here is all in a day's work for me."

She cocked her head. "What sort of work?"

"I'm a pilot."

"For one of the big airlines?"

"Nope. For whoever can afford me."

"Fascinating," Kennedy said. "I love planes."

He took the bait exactly the way she'd hoped. "I'd be happy to give you a tour through mine."

"I'd adore that." Kennedy set down her champagne glass. "Anything wrong with right now?"

"Not a thing."

His grin widened, suggesting perhaps she'd been playing into his hands, not the other way around, and a secret thrill shot through her at the challenge. "Night, girls and boy." Kennedy linked her arm through Sam's, conscious of his tautly muscled forearm and the way the heat of his skin ignited sparks of awareness in all the appropriate places.

She gave an approving sigh as he settled her into his Lamborghini, fastened her seat belt, then leaned in close to her. "We could skip the airport and go straight to my place."

"Sam Watson, what makes you think I'm that kind of girl?"

"Las Vegas, March 2005. You were with Jamir. I was your pilot."

"Oh."

"I was flying my old plane back then."

"In that case we should definitely go see your new plane."

"If you insist."

As Sam drove, Kennedy studied his profile in the lights from the dashboard. From a square-chiseled masculine jaw, to a nose too crooked to be considered pretty, to those full sexy lips, everything about him screamed confident and capable.

"Jamir was in a bad mood that weekend," she said finally. "He hates to lose."

"Is that why he flew back alone?"

"I was having fun and wasn't ready to leave yet, so I didn't."

"He sent me back for you a few days later, but you weren't there."

She smiled sweetly. "I caught a different ride back."

"I can't express just how disappointed I was. I'd been looking forward to having you all to myself."

She leaned forward so her breasts lightly brushed his arm. "Careful what you wish for."

He flashed her a megawatt smile. "Now, what fun would careful be?"

Ignoring the temptation to glance at her travel clock, Justine rose and tugged a light silk robe over her short nightie before she left the villa. Judging from the ink-dark sky, it was still the wee hours.

Their villa backed onto the seventeenth hole and she found her way there barefoot, enjoying the sensation of cool, dew-dampened grass underfoot.

She knew perfectly well why she couldn't sleep. She was wracked by her own stupidity, and the fact that she was more her mother's daughter than she cared to admit.

Her mother had always been open about her love affair with the married man who disappeared the second he learned Justine was on the way, and Justine had sworn she'd never make that same mistake. The only bright spot was that she now understood her mother a little better. How easy to kid yourself that he loved you more, that he'd leave her one day. When her mother tried to force the issue by getting pregnant, that was the end of the man and the beginning of her mother's downhill slide.

In the midst of her musings, she heard a click just as a stream of cold water hit her full on. She shrieked, frozen in shock.

She didn't see the stranger approach from the shadows and barely felt a tug on her arm before she found herself swept up into strong arms.

Out of sprinkler range, the man set her down by a golf cart as carefully as if she was fragile crystal. He pushed her sodden brown hair back and tilted her head up to meet her eyes.

"What are you doing out here? Are you all right?"

"I'm fine, I . . ." Justine looked up into kind, concerned gray eyes and had the overwhelming urge to bury her head against that warm, strong chest.

Then she realized she could get a head start on her two fellow contestants, who were still asleep. Her competitive streak rose as she tried to recall the sexcapades list. Making love outdoors sprang to mind.

"How embarrassing," she murmured. "I must have been sleepwalking." Her gossamer robe was drenched and clung to every curve, while her nightie might as well have been transparent.

She took a deliberately unsteady step and managed to brush against her companion. "I hope you didn't get all wet rescuing me." She smoothed a hand down the front of his golf shirt, where powerful pecs couldn't disguise the rapid beat of his heart.

"Did you sleepwalk far?" He frowned as if wondering what he was supposed to do with her.

"I'm not sure," she fibbed. "What brings you out here at this time of night?"

"A superintendent's day starts early. Do you know your name?"

"I'm Justine Bates," she said. "I just arrived here from Seattle."

He chuckled. "I hope you didn't sleepwalk all that way."

She joined his laughter. Seattle and Mr. Married suddenly seemed a long way away, and she was liking where she'd wound up.

"Are you used to rescuing damsels in damp distress?"

"At first I thought that you might be a ghost. You never know what kind of early settlement might have been here generations before the course was built."

"I hope you're not disappointed to learn I'm just flesh and blood." She hugged herself, sleeking the sheer gown tightly against her curves.

"Disappointed wouldn't be the word. But I have to confess I'm at a loss as to what to do next."

Justine moved flush against him. "How about a nice, big thank-you kiss for rescuing me?"

"That sprinkler *was* pretty dangerous," he murmured, lowering his head till his lips were a scant inch from hers. His hands settled on her waist, warming her skin.

"I was frozen with fear," Justine said, just as his lips met hers and her pulse leapt with delirious happiness.

Chapter Two

*H*e fit his hard body against Justine's with confident ease as he pulled her close. His hands cupped her backside, angling his hips in a way that told her how aroused he was.

Her response was so swift and so automatic it shocked her. Her handsome stranger was *exactly* what she needed, and she reached out for more.

His mouth worked magic against hers and she locked her hands behind his head, holding him there. When she parted her lips, their tongues mated and she shivered, despite the way he was heating her up from the inside out.

"You must be cold in those wet things," he said when they finally came up for air.

"Perhaps I should get out of them."

"I agree." His fingers fumbled with the robe's belt and she found his clumsiness more endearing than if he'd disrobed her with ease. He pushed the wet fabric off her shoulders and peeled it down to puddle at her feet. His large hands followed the fabric's journey, his palms reverently smoothing and caressing every inch of her.

"Your skin is amazingly soft." The backs of his knuckles grazed her breasts through the thin, damp fabric of her nightie and her nipples tightened pleasurably, zinging their approval to the sweet spot near her V Zone.

"That feels *so* good, " she said breathily.

Cupping her breasts, he pleasured her nipples with his thumbs, warming them through the dampness.

Impatiently, she untucked his shirt and slid her hands up the wall of his chest, then moved closer so her breasts rubbed his chest, stimulated by the crisp matting of hair.

He slid his hand underneath her nightie, fingers honing in to stroke that hot, needful place.

A jolt of sensation shot straight through her and she clutched his shoulders for support as she rode his hand. She'd never expected to feel this again, this mindless oblivion to everything but her body's response. The inner fire consumed her as her body started to tighten in anticipation, her inner lips swollen and dampened by the rush of her desire.

"Turn around and lean against here."

She held on to the back of the golf cart and let him angle

her body as he nudged up behind her, teasing her, inflaming her. When he finally pushed inside her she sobbed in pleasure at the way they fit together, their bodies' rhythms feeding and fueling each other in the dark before dawn.

He grasped her hips for leverage, increasing the friction and the pace. Gasping sobs of pleasure rocked her as her orgasm spiraled through her and his propelled her on to greater heights.

Lisa was falling way behind already; she just knew it. First Kennedy left with that gorgeous pilot last night. Then Justine showed up this morning with her robe on inside out, wrinkled and grass-stained, and a dazed and rapturous look on her face.

Lisa tucked a chunk of baby-fine blonde hair behind her ear as she studied her sexcapades list. "Can we talk about this?"

Kennedy laughed. "I kept it pretty tame."

"Does it count if each item takes place with the same man?"

"I don't think we need a lot of detailed rules—just go with the flow. What do you think, Just?"

"Hmm . . ." Justine glanced up and blinked as if pulled from a lovely daydream.

"If any of us meets someone right away and gets them to play along, it's not much of a contest, is it?" Lisa said.

"Lisa, you're taking this all too seriously," Kennedy said. "The whole idea is to have fun. Don't pick an apple on your first walk around the orchard. Take your time, smell the fruit, and sample any pieces that catch your fancy."

"I'm getting dressed." Lisa pushed back her chair abruptly. She was being a pain and she knew it. But it was easier for the others, neither of whom had been married and betrayed by the one she trusted the most. At age thirty-two, she wondered if she'd ever trust again.

By the time they reached the golf course, Lisa had managed to pull herself together. It was a glorious day, the temperature already in the mid 70s, and she was glad they'd elected to golf early. She was on vacation, she reminded herself as she sifted through the cute golf outfits in the pro shop.

"Ready?" Kennedy asked.

"More than ready," Lisa said.

Two golf carts were parked outside the pro shop and she headed for the closest one and put her clubs on the back, aware that Kennedy had stopped to talk to a tall, nicely dressed man carrying an expensive-looking set of clubs. That girl never missed a beat. Why couldn't she be more like that?

"Lisa, Richard will be our pro today, giving us pointers on our game."

She suddenly found herself face to face with the man who'd tucked the flower behind her ear last night. Drowning in that familiar, admiring gaze, she stiffened.

"Hello again, Lisa."

"Hi, yourself." Behind them, she was vaguely aware of her two friends climbing into the second golf cart.

"Shall we?" He took her arm and guided her toward the cart.

For the life of her, Lisa couldn't think of a single thing to say.

"I didn't know you were a pro," she blurted out as they headed down the course, following the other two to the first hole. "I thought you were a tourist."

"One of the idle rich?" He laughed. "Most of the men who vacation here would trade places with me in a second. They'd die happy to have been a golf star."

"Should I have recognized you last night?"

"I'm no Tiger Woods, but I did all right."

"And you give lessons?"

"Among other things."

"What other things?" Lisa asked curiously.

"I design courses. More recently, I've written a book."

Why couldn't she be attracted to someone more ordinary? Why did she have to be drawn to a celebrity?

"I'm not a very good golfer," she said, knowing she'd be a whole lot worse with him watching her.

"Don't worry about that. I'm just rounding out your foursome, really."

Sure he was. Lisa sighed heavily. "You were kind to me last night. But you were wrong about me being sad."

"Lisa, you don't have to explain anything to me."

Interesting comment, since she'd spent a lifetime ensuring she wasn't misinterpreted. The way she'd been raised, everything had to look perfect at all costs. Even her totally flawed marriage.

"Did you arrange this today?"

He turned and rested his arm across the back of the bench seat, so close his fingertips nearly brushed her shoulder. "I met Kennedy when she was here before, and I figured last night that you were traveling with her. When I saw her name on the schedule, I took the open seat. I didn't trust fate to ensure that our paths would cross again while you were here, and I wanted them to. Very much," he added.

She stared straight ahead, weighing his words. She didn't use to be so suspicious, but Les's untrustworthy behavior had changed that.

But it was time to get over that. She had the sexcapades hunt to win! "I'm flattered."

The cart lurched to a stop at the first hole. "Speaking for myself, I'm enchanted."

Lisa smiled. What a lovely word.

"Did you set Richard up with Lisa?" Justine asked Kennedy as they followed the others to the next hole.

"Nope. One hundred percent his idea. But what a great chance for her to get over Loser Les once and for all."

"And how was Pilot Sam?" Justine continued. "As yummy as he looked?"

"Hmmm. Speaking of hookups, I noticed your inside-out grass-stained robe at breakfast."

Justine flushed. "I don't know what you're talking about."

Kennedy just laughed. "I'm betting Miles does."

They pulled up at the next hole and parked behind the other cart.

"Which club are you planning to use?"

"My three wood, unless Richard recommends something different."

"Good luck getting any advice out of him. I'd say his entire focus is on Lisa."

Lisa wasn't sure how her golf game ended up so well when she was totally distracted by Richard's presence the entire time. But it was impossible not to bask in his openly admiring attention.

Not that he wasn't perfectly professional, helping each of the girls improve their form and their score. But she was the one he'd asked out later, and after several hours spent in close proximity, her hormones were singing with anticipation as she joined the other girls for lunch.

"Day one and counting," Kennedy said, raising her martini to toast the others.

"Anyone else have a date tonight?" Lisa tried to act more cool than she felt.

"Apparently your day started off rather well," Kennedy said. "Let me guess. Richard?"

Lisa nodded, feeling her excitement bubbling up inside her. "He just feels like . . . I don't know exactly. Some sort of a kindred spirit."

Kennedy shook her head. "Lisa, there doesn't have to be a divine connection for you to sleep with the guy. Just have fun for once. Don't take life so seriously."

"I wasn't aware that I do."

Kennedy reminded herself to tread more lightly with her friends; they weren't as seasoned as her. She patted Lisa on the arm. "You are who you are, sweets. All I'm trying to say is, lighten up a little."

"Yeah," Justine said. "There's a lot to be said for the 'zip-less fuck.'"

"That phrase is a real flashback," Kennedy said with a chuckle. "Any particular reason you used it?"

Justine flushed under their scrutiny. "It just seems appropriate."

Kennedy smiled, pleased that her plan for helping her friends move on with their lives seemed to be working. Wait till they saw what other surprises were in store.

"Well, this afternoon I say we divide and conquer. Lisa, just because you have a date tonight doesn't mean the challenge for the rest of the day disappears."

"You are incorrigible."

"I try." Kennedy grinned.

Her friends would be shocked if they had the faintest idea of what happened last night. Sam had been the perfect gentleman. He'd shown her around his plane, chatted about a million different things, ignored her attempts to seduce him, and dropped her off at the villa without even a kiss.

A close scrutiny in the mirror this morning had assured her, that, even in her mid-thirties, she was as beautiful as ever. So what went wrong? Was she losing her touch? She knew for a fact that he wasn't gay, and that he found her attractive. It was almost as if he was determined not to be her plaything. For a girl who was accustomed to having men fall at her feet, it was an intriguing challenge. One she had every intention of following up on, even if it meant stowing away on his plane.

*   *   *

The girls parted ways after lunch, and Justine had just come out of the ladies' room when she found her way blocked by a large man.

"Justine, we need to talk."

A jolt of awareness shot through her. So much for the zipless fuck. "Oh."

"In here." He pulled her into an empty banquet room and closed the door. "I . . . uh . . ."

Apparently he was as much at a loss for words as she was, looking so ill at ease Justine wished she was just about any other place.

"Don't worry," she said. "Last night was just something that happened. No repeat performance expected." She forced a laugh. "I don't even know your name."

"Eric Mills. And despite what happened, I don't 'do' casual sexual encounters. I want you to know that."

"Thank you."

"Justine, we didn't use protection. I was totally caught up in the moment and didn't give it a thought. But I wanted you to know that I'm healthy and clean. And not promiscuous, despite my actions. I'm also not interested in becoming a father right now."

"You needn't worry. I'm healthy, too. And if I ever decide I want a child, it won't be from some random encounter with a stranger."

"Sorry, I . . ." He ran his fingers through his endearingly ruffled hair. "I started this all wrong. Will you have dinner with me tonight?"

"Why?" she asked warily.

"I'd like the chance to get to know you—the real woman behind the sexy object of my fantasies come to life."

"The fantasy is always better than the reality," she warned.

"In this instance, I doubt it very much." He stepped closer, tilted her chin up, and looked directly into her eyes. Justine felt her pulse kick into overdrive. But instead of the kiss she expected, he captured her hand, raised it to his lips, and kissed it. "See you tonight. I'll pick you up at seven."

"You don't know where I'm staying," Justine said.

"Oh, yes, I do," he said.

Which left Justine to wonder what else he knew about her.

The mechanic tinkering on Sam's plane had required very little persuasion to tell her where to find Sam, and Kennedy boldly headed through the pilot's lounge to the shower room as if it was something she did every day.

She followed the sound of running water to the tiled shower area, where the frosted glass door provided only a tease of the wet, naked man within.

To his credit, Sam didn't flinch when she opened the door and gazed at him admiringly. Instead, he passed her the soap.

"You're just in time to do my back." He turned and presented a tantalizing view of strong, muscular legs, and a tanned, sculpted back and shoulders above a pale, well-shaped backside. While it wasn't as tanned as his back and legs, his ass had clearly seen the light of day a time or two. Skinny-dipping perhaps?

His skin was warm and smooth beneath her palms as she guided the soap in slow circles across the slope of his shoulder blades, then down the indentation of his spine before she dropped the soap, leaving both hands free to cup his buttocks and squeeze.

Before she could get any more adventurous, he stepped away and turned the water off. Scooping his hair back with both hands he faced her, clearly comfortable with his nudity. "What would you have done if it wasn't me?"

"What do you think I'd do?" she asked in her most provocative tone.

Sam laughed and shook his head as he stepped out of the shower and grabbed a nearby towel. "I doubt you would have apologized."

"What would I have to be sorry for?"

"Taking so long to get here?" he said.

"That couldn't be helped. I'm a busy lady."

"I just bet you are." As he dried himself with brisk, economical movements, she was disappointed to see he wasn't aroused by the sight of her, a wrong she was determined to put right. But before she could make a move he'd stepped into his pants, zipped, and fastened them.

She frowned. This would have been the perfect opportunity to scoop his boxers, except he clearly wasn't wearing any. Which meant she'd have to recruit a new volunteer. No matter. There were other ways Sam could be of use to her.

"What's your hurry to get dressed?" she said.

"Like you, I'm a busy person."

She stepped forward and placed one hand on his chest, the other on the waistband of his pants. "Too busy for me?"

"That all depends what you have in mind."

"I was thinking about getting to know each other better." She ran her hand down the fly of his pants, gratified to feel him getting hard.

"Does anyone ever really know you, Kennedy?"

"*You're* welcome to try."

"I know you're used to going after what you want."

"I've found that to be the best way."

He captured both her hands and removed them so he could shrug into his shirt.

"You might try reining it in for a change. Let someone else make the first move."

"What if they don't make the move I'm looking for?"

"That's the chance you take."

"And if I don't like leaving things up to chance?"

He sat down and put on his socks and shoes. "One day, someone will come along who you can't control or manipulate. Then where will you be?"

She cocked her head as if considering his words. "It's an intriguing thought. A new experience?"

"Exactly, Princess. A new experience." He dropped a kiss to the top of her head as he moved past her.

He paused and turned at the door. "I have to fly a guy this afternoon but I should be back in time for a late dinner."

"What if I already have plans?"

"Change them." The door closed behind him.

Sam Watson was definitely a force to be reckoned with. And she knew exactly how to get started.

Justine

Sexcapades

collect:

— your date's boxers
— his favorite golf glove
— a snip of his chest hair

score:

— a shooter he slurps from your belly button
— an extravagant piece of jewelry
— a picture of his penis

enjoy:

— sex in a limo
✓ water sex (indoors or out) *does sprinkler count? I think so!*
✓ sex outdoors (double points for daytime)
— skinny-dipping with your date
— dress-up sex
— him as your slave, bondage included

Chapter Three

$\mathcal{L}$isa stretched in the warm sunshine and yawned contentedly as she slathered on another layer of sunblock. With her fair coloring, she had to be really careful not to burn.

"This is the life." Justine rolled over and spritzed herself with water from the spray bottle at her side.

"Pretty nice, having our own private pool," Lisa agreed. "I could get used to this lifestyle."

Justine propped herself up on one elbow. "I thought you were born to this."

Lisa nodded. "Sadly, so did I. It was only after I was married that I learned it was all show. My parents are mortgaged to the hilt. That's why they were so against any talk of divorce."

"Yikes!" Justine said. "I had no idea."

"Yeah," Lisa said. "I got life insurance when Les died, but I put it away to help take care of my folks."

"But the gallery's doing great, right?"

Lisa shrugged. "Not bad, but there are always slow times. Before, I had the security of Les to bail me out. Now it's all on my shoulders."

"And very capable shoulders they are." Justine sat up and shaded her brow to glance around. The pool deck was bordered on three sides by a waist-high concrete wall topped by verdant green foliage speckled with white blossoms. Beyond the hedge stood rows of identical villas, each with its own pool.

Lisa looked up at her. "What's wrong?"

"Nothing, really." Justine lay down again. "Just one of those eerie feelings, like maybe we're being watched."

"You're being watched by me." Kennedy breezed toward them. "Look at you two, lolling by the pool."

"You're in my sun." Lisa lazily blinked up at Kennedy who stood next to her, holding a raft of shopping bags. "What did you buy?"

"Oh, this and that," Kennedy said airily, perching on a chaise lounge and delving into her bags. "Wanna see?"

"Tools for seduction?" Justine asked.

"These are toys."

"Looks like tools to me," Lisa said, admiring the skimpy lingerie, sexy shoes, and slinky dress Kennedy shook free one at a time from their cocoon of bright green tissue paper.

"Sometimes a girl just has to pull out all the stops. And I'd like to make a slight amendment to the list. We should have one wild card—your choice of something individual and personal to the guy. When we tally up the scores you must say why you chose this particular item. Three-point bonus for the most original, determined by our score-keeper."

"You're on!" The three girls slapped hands in mid-air.

"Feels like time for a cold drink." Kennedy gathered up her purchases and went inside.

Lisa rose and dove into the pool.

Sometimes she felt like such a fraud around her two friends, who had far more life skills and experiences. She loved them both and sometimes wished she could be more easygoing like them.

The only child of older parents, she'd been expected to achieve an education, a husband, and a family, in that order. Even opening her own art gallery fit the overall plan—something suitable to occupy her days and make her well-rounded, but hardly a serious career. It had always been understood that her little business venture would take second place to the husband and family.

Her parents had been most disapproving of her and Les's separation, and it had been more for their sake than hers that she'd gone back, hurt that they preferred her married and miserable than divorced and happy.

Les's death in a freak skiing accident had come first as a shock, then as a relief. Widowhood was acceptable. Her behavior on this vacation certainly wasn't.

Could she even take part in this sexcapades hunt? She had to at least pretend. She couldn't let her friends down—or herself. She'd done too much of that lately. Like swallowing her pride and turning a blind eye to Les's infidelity, especially when he'd thrown it in her face.

She pulled herself out of the pool and went inside to get ready for her date. Things were about to change. So what if it had been forever since she'd been on a date? Get the man to talk about himself; wasn't that the age-old advice?

But apparently no one had cued Richard in, and as she sat across from him later that night, basking in the admiration of those kind gray eyes, she found herself chatting up a storm.

"Oh, listen to me." She finally ran out of steam. "Going on and on about trivial things. You've led a far more interesting life."

"I find what you do fascinating. Dealing with all those artists' personalities and egos."

"I doubt their egos are any different from a celebrity golfer's," she said, then bit her lip. "Oh, I didn't mean that the way it sounded."

To her relief, Richard laughed. "For the record, there was even ego involved in my retirement. I was determined to go out on top."

"But you didn't stay retired."

His eyes clouded slightly. "Too much time on my hands. I like what I'm doing now: designing courses, giving lessons, and I'm on the board of a charity. I just hope my book doesn't flop—my ego would have a hard time with that."

"I think it's amazing that you wrote a book."

"*Feng Shui Golf.*" He pulled a face. "My publisher's title; not mine."

"It seems nothing ever goes according to plan. You think you have this life course all mapped out and then wham-o, suddenly you're not just on the wrong road, you're on the whole wrong map and have to start all over again. The big U-turn in life."

"I don't think I've ever heard it put quite like that before," Richard said. When his hand slid across the table to cover hers it felt completely right and natural.

"So what was it like? Your golf-pro life?"

"When things went well, there was no better job in the world. I got to be out there doing what I loved."

"Adored by your fans," Lisa added.

"I had the best of all possible worlds. The excitement of being on tour, the challenge of the game, and the stability of the home and hearth waiting for me."

"It must have been hard to give it up."

"I left golf in an attempt to save my marriage," Richard said. "Turned out the marriage couldn't be saved. And my passion for the game faded at the same time."

Lisa nodded. "I understand about that type of sacrifice. How it seems right at the time."

"What's the expression? Two wrongs don't make a right?"

"But you still golf," Lisa pointed out. "And people know and recognize you. When we got to this restaurant, they knew your name. You have your own table."

"I can't deny there's something nice about feeling connected, no matter where I am in the world. Fancy a walk?"

"Sure." Lisa stood and he came up behind her and draped her shawl over her shoulders, smoothing its edges with his hands. She could feel the heat of his palms through the fabric, aware of the way it warmed her clear through. Gently, he turned her toward him.

Their surroundings faded away as if they didn't exist. The background clatter of other diners in a busy restaurant. Nothing existed beyond her and Richard. And the fact that she was dying to kiss him.

For a second she thought he felt the same and was going to act on it; then she heard his name called. He stepped away from her and greeted the newcomer, shaking the other man's hand, then introducing Lisa.

"Sorry about that," he said when they were finally alone together outside, having repeatedly turned down the other man's invitation to join him and his friends for a drink.

"You're like a rock star," Lisa teased. "I'd better get used to it."

Instantly, she wished she could take back her words. She sounded so presumptuous, taking for granted his interest in seeing her again.

He made no comment; he simply matched his step to hers and circled her shoulder with his arm in a way that made her feel precious and cherished. She snuck a sideways look at him.

How could she work down the sexcapades list when she couldn't even get the guy to kiss her?

"Do you know the people in that van?" she asked suddenly.

"What van?"

"That white one that just went past us. It's gone by a few times while we've been walking."

"Probably just some lost tourist." Richard said. "It's easy to get turned around out here." He pulled her close and she gave in to the temptation to rest her head on his shoulder.

"Contrary to what you might think, I never lived the celebrity lifestyle," he said. "No picking up groupies or trashing hotel rooms."

"Hmmm—there goes that van again," Lisa said. "Are you sure you're not married and your wife has put a private investigator on your tail?"

He blew out a breath and tugged her over to sit on a nearby bench, snugging her into the circle of his arm. As he spoke, he stroked her hair.

"My wife was very jealous and insecure. She never should have been married to someone who was away for months at a time. Despite everything I did to reassure her, she didn't believe I could possibly be faithful; she didn't think I could resist the temptations on tour."

"So the lack of trust eroded your marriage."

"It didn't help. But the kicker was when I arrived home un-expectedly and found her in bed with the pool boy." He tried to laugh. "Isn't that such a cliché? She tried to toss it back on me, like it was all my fault. We went for counseling but the damage was done. Especially when I learned he was one in a long string. In her mind I was out there playing around, so she retaliated in kind. It was no way to run a marriage."

Lisa sat quietly. They had more in common than he knew.

"Sorry," Richard said. "I didn't mean to dump all that stuff on you. But trust has become of tantamount impor-tance to me with everyone in my life."

"Understandable," Lisa said.

"Come on." He pulled her to her feet. "There's something I want to show you."

The golf course was deserted, the pro shop locked, but Richard pulled out keys, disarmed the alarm, and hustled her through to the display wall.

"These are some of my trophies." He unlocked the case and pulled one out. "They seemed so important at the time, but I would have traded them all for the chance to make my marriage work. That commitment to another person is real. This stuff is all just smoke and mirrors. It means nothing."

Lisa took the trophy from his hand, surprised by the cool weight of it. "It *is* real, Richard. It's proof of your talent, dedi-cation, and your accomplishments, and you shouldn't deni-grate that. As for your wife, she would have been jealous if you were tending bar or selling vacuums. That was her. This is you." She put the trophy back. "And this is you and me."

She cupped his face in her hands. It felt so good to focus

on someone else for a change. Richard had been kind to her from the outset, responding to her on some subliminal level she hadn't been aware of. He'd also been deeply hurt yet moved past it, gaining strength and compassion. Something it was her turn to do.

She traced the shape of his mouth, soft yet firm, and felt his lips tremble beneath her fingertips. She heard him exhale as his lips parted and she dipped her finger inside, dampened it. Teased him further till she leaned forward and allowed her lips to meet his.

Her mouth shaped his as her fingers had, tasted his flavor, absorbed him into her, tempering his hurt. The results were explosive. What started out as a soft, gentle, exploratory kiss quickly flared to an inferno of mutual need.

He was inhaling her, devouring her, starved for her, and for once she felt she could feed his need; a need that was far greater than hers.

She clutched his shoulders, his back, his behind, her hands running freely up and down his body as she rubbed against him, chest to chest, hip to hip, thigh to thigh.

That sexual side that she'd thought had died with her marriage roared to life with a vengeance. She heard moaning and realized it was her as he kissed and stroked and probed her softness: her neck, her shoulders, her back.

She felt his hands on her behind, tilting her pelvis, lifting her up and into him, locking her against his arousal and sending a rush of heated blood to her nether regions.

He was shimmying her dress up her legs, stroking every inch of bare skin he could, and she grew warm and moist, wanting more as his mouth continued to work its magic on hers. His tongue mated with hers as his hands stroked and shaped her breasts through the thin silk of her sheath. She felt her nipples harden into pressure points of further demand.

Her dress was ruched up around her waist, his hands inside the tiny wisp of thong underwear that was more enticement than barrier. He found her dampened need and stimulated her to heightened levels of desire, his talented fingers stroking and delving as he kissed her senseless.

He lifted her onto a display table, pushing the stacks of golf shirts aside, slid her panties off of her and out of the way, and nudged her legs farther apart, teasing the soft skin at the top of her thighs as he knelt before her.

His hands kneaded her legs, a strong yet gentle massage from knee to upper thigh, before he raised her legs to rest atop his shoulders and buried his face in her juicy ripeness.

He blew on her, his breath hot and arousing, followed by the softest lapping of his tongue, tracing and exploring her shape. She felt herself unfold and open, warm and wanton as the first tiny ripples of pleasure seeped through her.

"Oh, Richard." It was both an epiphany and a plea for more as she tangled her fingers through his hair and held his head.

He added his own murmurs of pleasure as he licked and tasted and enjoyed her.

Lisa was beyond thought, a knot of tension building deep within her and radiating outward, first in slow motion, then with accelerated speed until everything exploded.

She lay boneless, gasping for air, the tremors still ricocheting through her. When her senses slowly regathered, she realized her hands were still tangled in Richard's hair.

Slowly she released him. He rose to his feet, stuffed her panties in his pocket, and smiled down at her in supreme satisfaction. "That was the perfect nightcap."

Chapter Four

$\mathscr{H}$aving watched Justine leave with Eric, and Lisa skip off with Richard, Kennedy was left feeling the walls of the villa closing in on her. Sam had been so damn sure she'd be here waiting for him, it would serve him right if she wasn't. Except the man intrigued her.

"Why so restless?" Miles asked as she picked up a fashion magazine and tossed it back down again.

"I'm just not accustomed to waiting around for anyone," Kennedy said.

Miles's eyes twinkled. "He does seem like the confident, take-charge type."

"He's a little *too* sure of himself." Just then her cell phone rang and she leapt for it.

"Yes. Yes, exactly. I'll confirm later. Right." She flipped the phone closed and stared at it with a frown.

"What are you up to, Kennedy?" Miles asked.

"A little surprise for the others."

He raised a brow.

"Don't look at me like that. And don't worry, you'll be handsomely rewarded when this is done."

"It's not *me* that I'm worried about, my dear. It's you."

"Worrying about me is a waste of time." Her comment was punctuated by the doorbell's chime. "That would be my date. Could you be a love and let him in?"

Artfully she arranged herself on the plush, super-suede sofa, the open magazine on her lap, which she pushed aside as Miles ushered Sam into the room. She rose and went to his side, where she tilted her head to study him.

"You look tired. Would you like a drink or something to eat?"

"I'm fine. We hit some weather and had to reroute."

Kennedy circled her lips with her tongue and laid a hand against his chest, encouraged to feel the leap of his heart. Sam was nowhere near as unaffected by her presence as he pretended to be. "I didn't mind waiting for you."

He laughed aloud. "Liar! You hate to wait. Doesn't she, Miles?"

Miles mimicked a zipper closing across his lips and left the room.

"I have no doubt you'll make the wait worthwhile," Kennedy teased.

"I'll do my best." He pulled her to him and kissed her long and deep while his hands roved her shape, his actions, his hard body all letting her know he had every intention of calling the shots.

My my, Kennedy thought as she slipped from his embrace and went to the bar. *This promises to be most interesting.*

"I thought you might be too tired to go out to eat, so I had Miles fix one of his specialties in case you'd rather stay in." Without asking, Kennedy poured him a fifteen-year single-malt Glenfiddich neat, then refilled her wineglass.

He nosed the scotch and raised an approving brow. "Lucky guess as to my favorite brand?"

"One of the many talents of a good PR person," Kennedy said smoothly.

She sashayed toward him, took his hand in hers, and led him to the couch facing the pool. In the dark, the underwater lights gave the pool an otherworldly glow. She curled her legs beneath her and leaned against him. "I've been thinking about you all day."

"That's nothing," Sam said. "I've been thinking about you for years."

Kennedy laughed. "We're going to have fun together, aren't we?"

"I have very little doubt of that." He tossed back the last of his drink and rose to his feet. "You'll want to change those shoes."

Kennedy extended one foot to admire her shiny new red stilettos. Having spent forever wrapping the satin ribbons around her ankles and adjusting the bows, she had no intention of taking them off. Not even when her legs were wrapped around Sam's gorgeous body.

"I don't think so."

He shrugged. "It's up to you. Come on."

"Where are we going?"

"It's a surprise." He leaned in close and ringed her lips with the blunt tip of his index finger. "Don't tell me you're not accustomed to surprises. Surely you're not *always* in control?"

She pushed out her lower lip as he played with it. "My surprises usually come in small, tastefully wrapped jewelers' boxes."

Sam laughed. "Stick with me." Still flung across the chair was the scarf he'd returned the other evening, and he picked it up. "The scarf that started it all. How fortuitous."

Before Kennedy had any clue as to his intentions, he covered her eyes and tied it behind her head as a makeshift blindfold. "Let's make this a little more interesting, shall we?"

Kennedy giggled. This was more like it. "Where are you taking me?"

"I told you, it's a surprise." He led her out of the villa, settled her into the passenger seat of his car, and they roared off into the night. Kennedy rested her hand on Sam's strong thigh, feeling the flex of muscles as he accelerated. She walked her fingers higher, aware of a rush of excitement she hadn't felt in a long, long time. She was accustomed to men falling at her feet the second she crooked her finger, and she could tell there'd be no finger-crooking with Sam. But she did have a surprise or two of her own.

They hadn't driven very long before he pulled the car to a stop and turned off the motor. She heard him rummaging behind him for something before he got out and went around to open her door and help her from the car. "First stop," he said. "Any guesses?"

She sniffed, aware of the way her other senses were heightened without sight. "Very outdoorsy," she said. "Night smells. Yet it's quiet. No other traffic. Did you bring me someplace intimate so you could ravish me?"

"Close," Sam said. "I brought you someplace I could challenge you."

With his arm around her, he guided her from the car. The ground became noticeably rougher underfoot and she was rethinking her footwear by the time he stopped and removed her blindfold.

"Ta-dah!" Sam said.

In the uneven terrain, she saw what appeared to be a hodgepodge of weird lights and shadowy shapes. "We're in the middle of nowhere."

"Not exactly nowhere. We're on a Frisbee golf course."

"Is this some sort of joke?" Hands on hips, she faced him, not sure if she should laugh or stomp her foot. "Do I look like a Frisbee golf type of girl?"

"I'm pretty sure you can be whatever you put your mind to."

The surrounding area was slightly hilly, scattered with free-standing targets and illuminated by colorful spotlights.

A pond lit by underwater lights shimmered in the distance as a fountain of spray shot upward, the whole ringed by shadowy foliage.

"I challenge you to a game." Sam opened his quiver and offered her a choice of glow-in-the-dark discs. "Winner calls the shots, loser acquiesces. You win, you get to do whatever you want with me. And vice versa."

Kennedy reached for a Frisbee. "I'll be red. And I'm warning you, I used to throw a mean Frisbee back in the day."

"I'm betting you still can."

Kennedy tapped her chin with a long fingernail. "Let's make this more interesting."

"What do you have in mind?"

"We could play strip Frisbee golf."

Sam laughed. "Nice try, but I'm not letting you distract me that easily. You'll have to beat me fair and square."

"If you insist." Kennedy stepped onto the plate and took aim at the first target. She knew she wouldn't hit it, but at least hoped to throw straight. She watched her disc sail through the air in completely the wrong direction, followed by a loud splash as it landed in the pond.

"Oops." She turned and selected a bright neon pink one. "Practice round," she said. "This one's for real." She felt a small charge of satisfaction as the disc flew through the air, straight toward the target. It landed short, but ought to be an easy "birdie."

"Nice throw," Sam said, taking aim and following her course.

"Are we the only ones here?" Kennedy asked.

"We are."

"How did you arrange that?"

"It's all a matter of who you know," Sam said smugly.

"And here I thought you didn't want to be alone with me." Her disc hit the target with a satisfying clink as it landed in the metal basket.

"What gave you that idea?"

"Every time we're alone, it seems like you've got someplace you need to be."

"And you're accustomed to being the sole focus of a man's attention."

"That *is* how it tends to work."

"And exactly the way you like it."

She stopped and cocked her head to one side. "I can't figure you out, Sam Watson."

She saw the white flash of his grin in the dim light. "Fascinates you, doesn't it?"

"Actually, your arrogance and conceit appal me."

"Which doesn't stop you from coming back for more," Sam pointed out.

"Ha—you all but kidnapped me this evening. Where's the next target?"

"Why do I get the feeling it's me?"

"Fore!" She flung the Frisbee wildly, not really watching her aim, gratified to see Sam duck out of the way. He reached her in two strides, caught and manacled her right wrist.

"You've got a wild aim there, Kennedy. Be careful!"

She tried to jerk her arm free. His hold tightened.

As they faced off in the moonlight, Kennedy felt desire ripple through her, radiating outward from Sam's grip on her wrist.

"Are you going to play nice?"

"Never. Nice girls finish last."

"And Kennedy James plays to win."

"By whatever means are available." She grinned.

"Tell you what," he said. "I'll piggyback you around the course so you don't ruin those impractical shoes of yours."

Sam turned and squatted so Kennedy could clamber aboard, her arms around his shoulders, her legs wrapping his waist. It wasn't quite the pose she had envisioned earlier this evening, but it was definitely a step in the right direction.

He knew his way around the course and didn't seem at all bothered by her added weight. Kennedy had to admit it was fun as they made their way from target to target, snugged up against Sam, her breasts pressed against his back, her nipples tingling at the stimulation of movement. Every time he put her down she slid a little more slowly, their bodies meshed together in the slow glide of foreplay.

The game took them through a pirate ship, behind a waterfall, and across a stream in a miniature canoe. Sam played more skillfully than she did, easily taking the lead, yet when they finally reached the ninth hole she was almost sorry the game was over.

"That was fun," she said as Sam packed up their discs. "More than I thought."

"You don't usually let yourself play, do you?"

"What do you mean? I play the game of life."

"I was watching you tonight. It took you a while to forget about winning or losing, to just have fun."

"You don't know me at all."

"I know a little. Enough to know you're up to something on this trip."

"What a suspicious mind you have. It's just a vacation with my girlfriends."

"No, it's not. It's more than that."

Because he was studying her far too closely for her peace of mind, Kennedy changed the subject. "Since you won the game, what are you planning to do with me?"

"I'm going to cook you dinner. At my place."

"You cook?" Kennedy cooed. "Excellent. Research has proven that men who cook make the best lovers."

"Of course," Sam said, his hand on the small of her back as they returned to his car. "Because cooking is about appreciation for all things sensual."

As Eric drove, Justine couldn't help sneaking glances at him. How was it possible to have sex with someone and not know him at all?

Eric didn't say much, leaving her free to concentrate on the breathtaking scenery.

"How big is the island? It looked pretty small from the air."

"It's about twelve miles long and five miles wide. It used to be owned by a family named Walker, hence the name."

"You must find it somewhat confining when you live here."

"It's a bit of a goldfish bowl."

"How did you wind up here?"

"My ex-wife worked in the hotel industry. Since I'm able to work anyplace that people golf, we moved around a lot to build her career. The good thing about a place like this is that the visitors are all in vacation mode. Generally they're happy to be here and easy to be around. The downside is the high cost of living and there's very little privacy. I got tired of moving around, so here I am. What do you do back in Seattle?"

"I'm an interior designer."

"That's a competitive racket. You must be good."

"I am," Justine said. No ego, simply stating a fact. "Where are we headed?"

"Since you're from the west coast, I figured you'd like the water. We can go out on my boat and eat dinner while I show you the island from a different vantage point."

Eric parked at the marina and unloaded a cooler and picnic backpack from his black SUV. Justine commandeered the backpack and followed him along the slip to where a beautiful cabin cruiser tugged at her mooring ropes.

"She's beautiful."

"Yeah, she has pretty lines. You know much about boats?"

"Beyond the fact that they float, very little. I've designed a few interiors to create maximum efficiency in a small space, so I'll be interested to see the cabin layout."

As Justine prepared to climb aboard, Eric caught her hand in his and steadied her. "I've been looking forward to this all day." He kept hold of her hand as she met his gaze.

She paused, then asked, "How long has it been since your divorce?" She needed to know for her own peace of mind.

He kept his gaze steady, as if reassuring her she could ask anything she needed to. "Three years."

"Does your ex-wife still live here?"

"She does; she's remarried. Her husband is a good guy."

That all sounded fairly healthy. "I didn't mean to give you the third degree, but a lot of men say they're separated, and all it really means is their wife isn't here right now."

Eric grinned. "Really? They say that?"

"All the time. It seems to be some code among the married ones who cheat."

"Anne and I tried really hard to make it work, but some of the obstacles were just too big to overcome. I haven't been involved with anyone else, other than the occasional date."

When Justine started to pull away, he tightened his hold. "I meant what I said before. You were like something out of a dream when I first saw you. I hope you don't have any regrets."

"Sometimes it's better to just get caught in the moment. No past, no future, no expectations."

"Can we continue to do that? Be in the moment?"

Justine nodded. "I'll try."

Still keeping her hand in his, he helped her down the narrow ladder-like staircase to the galley, where he opened a chilled bottle of Prosecco and filled two glasses. "Here's to being in the moment."

"To the moment," Justine echoed.

Chapter Five

Out of respect for the *Special T*'s well-tended decks, Justine slipped off her Jimmy Choo heels and made herself comfortable while Eric started the motor, cast off the mooring ropes, then steered the vessel from its slip. He moved with a confident ease, as if he and the boat were one fluid unit. He was even more good-looking in the sunlight, and she could happily feast her eyes on him for hours

He must have felt her gaze at some point for he looked directly at her. "There's a jacket on the back of the door downstairs if you start to get chilly."

"It's perfect," Justine said. "But thanks." She lowered her gaze to his hands and got an immediate thrill, recalling those hands on her body. Heat that had nothing to do with the balmy evening temperature flooded her veins.

He followed the journey of her eyes. "Want to know the real reason I brought you boating?"

"So it's not just an island tour?"

"This way I'm forced to concentrate on being a skipper. I was afraid I wouldn't be able to keep my hands off you otherwise."

Justine smiled a secret smile. Sexcapades victory, here she came!

She got up to stand next to him at the wheel. "Surely a man of your diverse talents is no stranger to multitasking."

He put his free arm around her waist and she moved in closer.

"I know a great little private cove where I thought we could eat while we watch the sun go down."

"Sounds wonderful." Justine couldn't believe how comfortable she felt leaning against Eric, the breeze ruffling her hair, enjoying the briny smell of the ocean. As they clipped across the waves, Eric filled her in on the history of the area, which was first inhabited by pirates and their cohorts on the wrong side of the law.

"How did the Walker family end up owning the island?"

"Walker was a famous gambler in the late 1700s and friends with the governor. Legend has it that the governor signed the island over to him in a poker game. Anyone who questioned the authority of the transaction mysteriously disappeared. Future generations of Walkers settled the island, establishing roads and a desalination plant and importing a lot of the tropical plants you see here today."

"What a great spot for pirates—all these hidden coves and waterways." Justine couldn't seem to stop riffling her fingers through his wavy brown hair. It was soft and springy to the touch, and it felt perfectly natural to play with it when her hand wasn't resting comfortably on his shoulder.

Suddenly she was aware of a boat keeping its distance behind them. Had it been there since they left the marina?

"May I use your binoculars for a second?"

"Sure."

She checked out the boat behind them, another pleasure craft ferrying a man and a woman. "Do many people know about this secret cove of yours?"

"I'm sure many do. Why?"

"It's just . . ." She passed him back the binoculars. "No reason." She'd learned to become suspicious when she was with Mr. Married, always wondering if his wife was having them followed. But there was no reason to suspect they were being followed. The couple on the other boat was undoubtedly out for a relaxing evening cruise the same as they were.

"That's our destination ahead," Eric said.

Justine picked up the binoculars and followed the line of Eric's index finger. The cove really was secret. One minute she saw nothing but craggy shoreline, the next they had passed into another world. High cliffs on either side of the cove stood sentry and guaranteed no one could surprise them. No other boats were anchored there. She was glad

Eric had sought her out. She could tell herself she was only here because of the sexcapades hunt. The truth was, the actual hunt was for her real self, the one she'd sublimated all those years she wasted on Mr. Married.

Eric stopped the engine and dropped anchor.

"What can I do?" Justine asked.

"Just relax and be my lovely guest." He fetched the cooler and picnic pack, bringing out a selection of cheeses and pâté, grapes, a baguette, and a bottle of Rhone wine.

"This looks amazing!"

Eric shrugged modestly. "I'd like to take credit but really can't. I know a good caterer and I asked her to pack me up a fantasy picnic with seduction in mind."

"You told her that?"

"I had to. She's used to packing me lonely bachelor meals, and has been lecturing me about getting out more."

"She must have been thrilled. She went all out." Justine peeked into a container of fat, feta-stuffed olives, and another with fresh figs. "I take it the divorce was amicable," she added with what she hoped was the right amount of casual interest.

Eric was busy opening the wine and his movements didn't falter as he filled a glass and passed it her way.

"There was no animosity, only sadness. I think the counselor was relieved when we finally called it quits, even if her bank account took a hit."

"Why do you say that?"

"If there was ever such a thing as trying too hard, that was Anne and I." He tipped the rim of his glass to hers. "We were both high achievers. When she failed to get pregnant at the time she deemed suitable, she took it as a personal failure. And that was the beginning of the end."

"Did she see a specialist?" Justine asked.

"Several," Eric said. "I can't pretend to understand what it feels like when a woman wants a child with every fiber of her being, but it became an obsession that slowly killed what we had. After that, we only made each other miserable."

"I'm sorry." Justine reached across and gave his hand a squeeze.

"No, I'm sorry. I didn't mean to bore you with my sad tale."

"There's no chance of that."

They both sat quietly, absorbing the serenity that surrounded them, no sounds other than the gentle lap of the ocean against the boat and the occasional cry of a seabird.

"How did you know I was a picnic girl?" Justine asked.

"How could you possibly not love a picnic?" He spread caviar on a toast round and held it toward her. "Open."

Without hesitation, Justine parted her lips to feel the brush of his fingers as he placed the morsel in her mouth. She playfully nipped at his fingers, then closed her lips around his fingertips and sucked gently. When she finally released him, he licked his fingers.

"I also have barbequed duck breast in a sour cherry sauce, a rice pilaf salad, triple cream Brie, vine-ripened tomatoes, and fresh fruit with crème fraîche and chocolate croissants for dessert."

"The way to a girl's heart."

"The heart wasn't my primary goal." He grinned.

She threw a piece of bread at him. "I'm going to be full and fat."

"I have the cure for that, as well."

"Oh, really?" She loved this. The easy banter, the silly antics, something she'd missed all those years she wasted as the "other woman."

"A refreshing dip in the ocean as the sun sets."

"But I didn't bring a bathing suit."

"You don't need one."

"I haven't skinny-dipped in years." She'd been thinking about counting the sprinkler incident as water sex, but this would be an even better adventure.

"So what's the occasion of you girls visiting Walker Hook?"

"Kennedy decided to surprise us." She deliberately left out her own recent defining point of change in her life.

"Any other reason?"

"It's been a challenging year professionally, lots of growth and change," she said. "And since you've been so candid, I'll add that I've just ended a long-term relationship."

"Happily?" Eric asked.

"It was my choice," Justine said ambiguously.

Eric rose and hunkered down in front of her. "I don't expect you to tell me anything you don't want to. I just want you to know that I'm really glad you're here with me." He leaned forward and brushed her lips with his. When he started to pull back Justine leaned in, gripped his shirtfront, and hung on for more. As he deepened the kiss she felt some tiny inside part of herself, a part she didn't even know had been frozen solid, begin to slowly thaw. The sensation left her positively light-headed.

When Eric slowly stood she followed, dragging her body up his, enjoying every place his male hardness met her female softness, wanting, needing, more. He was managing to touch her in ways she'd never been touched before, the physical sensations heightened by the thrill of emotions.

"I was afraid you'd have the entirely wrong impression about me. That I was . . . I don't know. . . . No stranger to middle-of-the-night sex romps with someone I didn't even know," she said.

His hand cradled the side of her head and she nestled into his touch. "I just thought we were following our instincts. Doing what felt right and natural at the time."

"I like what we're doing now," she said softly.

"Me, too."

As they finished their picnic, it seemed the sky was showing off solely for them, pulling out every color in the spectrum. Justine oohed and ahhed so much she felt like a broken record, and Eric laughed indulgently at her enthusiasm.

She was happy, Justine suddenly realized. With Mr. Married she'd always tried to be something she thought he wanted, something different from his wife. With Eric she felt totally free to just be herself.

"How about that swim you promised me?"

"Sunset swims are the best," Eric said.

"Just strip down and jump in?" Justine asked, feeling suddenly shy, glancing around as if to assure herself they really were alone.

"There're towels in that locker over there."

Justine resisted the urge to leave her underwear on. She'd thought Eric might do the gentlemanly thing and look away as she stripped out of her dress, but his eyes freely feasted on her as she stepped out of her clothes, hanging on to a towel for modesty's sake.

"You are so beautiful," he said. The sincerity in his voice and his gaze gave her the courage to slowly lower the towel.

He heaved a mighty sigh. "We'd better get in the water before I change my mind."

In mere seconds they were both down the ladder and over the side of the boat. The water felt like liquid silk against her skin. She hadn't swum in the sea for years and had forgotten how buoyant the salt water made her feel, like a just-released cork from a bottle of wine.

She temporarily lost sight of Eric when he dove under, only to pop up alongside her. He tossed his hair off his face with an unself-conscious gesture and pulled her toward him. He grabbed a rung of the boat's ladder to steady them.

How natural to anchor her hands atop his shoulders for balance, wrap her legs around his waist, and let him support her. Her breasts grazed the hair-spangled contours of his chest, the crisp hairs teasing her sensitive nipples into responsive pleasure points that felt hardwired to her womanhood.

Eric cupped her breast in his palm, adding his own magic friction to the mix. She felt a pleasurable rush of heated warmth at the apex of her thighs as he growled low in his throat and plundered the side of her neck with his hot mouth, tonguing the sensitive cord, nibbling that responsive spot where neck joined shoulder.

Her head fell back, eyes half-closed, awash in the pleasure of his touch, his presence, wanting him with an intensity she hadn't wanted anything in a very long time.

He reached between them, his fingers honing in on her throbbing, needful portal. Instead of heading straight for the sweet spot, he made a leisurely perusal of her womanly assets, further teasing and inflaming her.

The more she wriggled closer, silently begging for release, the more he seemed to enjoy teasing her.

Her breath rose and fell in harsh accompaniment to the ocean lapping against the side of the boat, matched by Eric's labored breath as she explored every reachable inch of his strong shoulders and upper arms, tight glutes and abs.

In a bold move she reached down and grasped his erection, using the water as a lubricant to glide her cupped palm lovingly up its pulsing hard length.

"No fair." But he laughed as he said it, his lips nipping at hers in a teasing kiss.

"All's fair," Justine said, bringing the velvety tip within grazing distance of her heated chalice. "Giving up the control?"

"Why should I give up a thing?"

She guided him toward her clit, groaned softly when his rigid heat made contact, and tightened her legs around him for leverage as she manipulated him to be her love toy. She rode just the tip, increasing her pace to a frenzied crescendo that burst into a much-needed orgasm.

With a sigh of surrender she collapsed against Eric, trusting him not to let her go as she sagged against him, her heart racing alongside his.

With her snugged against him like a barnacle on a rock, he helped her up the ladder ahead of him.

On board, he draped the towel across her shoulders as she lowered herself to the padded bench seat.

Then he knelt before her and gently pushed her legs apart, exposing her to the night air and his hungry, appreciative gaze.

"Mmm . . ." Justine's clit throbbed as he leaned forward and blew lightly, sending her into over-the-top combustion. Then he rose to her breasts, loving and laving each nipple in a leisurely fashion, his talented tongue tracing their shape as his strong mouth and lips tugged greedily.

"Beautiful, perfect breasts," he murmured. Cupping them reverently in his palms, he brushed his thumbs against nipples still moist from the dampness of his kiss.

Then he returned to her pleasure palace, his lips and tongue continuing their magic exploration. Soft undulating waves of delight radiated out through her, each tiny tremor like a mini orgasm building atop the previous ones, until she felt an uncontrollable, final crescendo of shattering proportions.

He rode it with her, gentling his actions as he absorbed the aftershocks of her pleasure. Then he held her as she basked in the afterglow.

"So," he said as her breathing returned to near normal. "Think you might be ready for me?"

Chapter Six

*W*as she ready for him? Justine felt she'd been waiting all her life for Eric, but she didn't dare say it aloud, let alone expect he might feel the same incredible connection.

"Don't tell me we're going to do it in a bed?" she teased as he led the way belowdecks. "How unimaginative."

"It's just a bunk; we'll have to save the real bed for some other time." He rubbed his hands across her back. "You're getting cold." He pulled back the duvet. "Slide in. I'm right behind you." Then he fumbled in a box near the bed and pulled out a condom.

"Thank you for caring about my health. What are you

doing now?" she asked as he slipped in next to her and studied the packets.

"Making sure they're not expired."

Justine smothered a giggle. "What would you do then?"

"Lucky for you, they're not."

"Lucky for *you*, you mean. I've already been well-pleasured."

"Hang on for more." He rolled atop her and fitted his body to hers as she yielded to his strength, absorbing his warmth. She ran her hands up the strong columns of his arms, enjoying the pull of taut muscle beneath her fingertips.

She exhaled breathlessly and pulled him down for a kiss, rearing back in surprise when his lips met hers. "Is that what I taste like?"

"Nectar of the goddesses," he said, taking her mouth and making it his, his tongue probing her sweetness.

"I think I ought to taste you for comparison's sake."

His eyes smiled into hers as he gave a mock sigh. "Very well." He knelt above her, the warm, pulsing strength of his erection on full display.

"Mmm." She wet her lips in anticipation as she stroked the strong columns of his legs, making him wait before she grasped his buttocks and drew him forward.

Her tongue darted out for light exploratory licks and nibbles from all directions before she made an O of her lips and ringed just the tip, while her tongue continued its gyrations. With him inserted barely an inch, she grasped his shaft and pumped him.

He pulled free in just a few moments, breathing hard. "Whoa! Time out!"

"Already?" Justine asked with a pout.

"I'm saving myself for the main event."

She stroked his cock and smiled when he jerked reflexively. "I have an idea."

"What's that?"

She licked her fingers and dampened the valley of her breasts, then pushed them together with him trapped between. "This might be fun."

"Are you kidding me?" He blew out a breath, slowly inserting and withdrawing, then returning, just as her tongue darted out. He groaned and shut his eyes. His breath sped up, keeping time with his pumping actions, as his hands covered hers and his thumbs teased her nipples.

"You like that?" she asked.

"You're amazing. Here I am trying to impress you with my control, and you're making it damn difficult."

He eased out of the valley of her breasts, grabbed a condom and rolled it over his straining erection, then eased into her.

Justine gave a sigh of pure delight at the way he fit and filled her, causing waves of pleasure to roll over her and undulate through her. His hands framed her face, watching her expression.

"Is that okay? Am I too heavy?"

Touched, she cinched her knees tight around his middle. "You feel absolutely perfect."

He stroked in and out, their bodies moving in a timeless rhythm that transcended all else. Justine's orgasm spiraled into his, then floated in the aftermath as her hands smoothed the muscled contours of his back. She absorbed the rise and fall of his breathing as he nuzzled her close.

For her, this was no zipless fuck. So, now what?

Kennedy followed Sam through the elevator doors into the tiled foyer of his penthouse. He clicked a master switch so the open-area living and kitchen space was bathed in subtle lighting that illuminated several large, modern works of art.

"Look around while I get dinner started," he said. "Do you like seafood?"

She let her gaze travel with lingering intent along his six-foot-plus frame. "I like *everything*."

He smiled a half smile that told her the message was received loud and clear.

She prowled from room to room, disappointed not to pick up one single clue about the "real" Sam Watson. The place was beautiful, if one wanted a glossy furniture ad.

"It's not natural living like this," she complained as she returned to the kitchen and watched him chop vegetables with military precision.

His eyes never left the task before him. "What's wrong with the way I live?"

"There's no clutter. Not even an unpaid bill or half-read magazine anywhere."

"I'm not here very much," Sam said as if that explained it.

"It doesn't look like you're ever here." Kennedy rose from her perch on the stool at the bar and continued to pace.

He set aside the knife. "You'd prefer it if I were a slob?"

"I'd prefer it if you weren't so damn perfect."

"Admit it: you'd also prefer it if I were a little more predictable, like your typical dates."

"You think you have me pegged, don't you?"

"First impressions last a long time."

"We need some music," Kennedy said abruptly. She'd bet his CDs were alphabetized.

He must have touched a hidden switch, because suddenly the soft strains of blues guitar music wafted through the air. Sam filled two wineglasses, then guided her out of the kitchen onto the wraparound balcony. It provided a perfect wide-angle view, the island lights winking below them, becoming more sparse as they reached the water.

"What's making you uncomfortable?" he asked, facing her. "Surely not me?"

"Who are you, Sam Watson?" she asked softly. "I need to know."

"Probably not like anyone you've met before."

She clicked her glass to his. "Nothing about you really adds up."

"It all adds up. I'm just not predictable, is all."

"One of the reasons I'm so good at PR is my ability to read other people. With you, I feel like I've opened a book and it's not written in English."

Sam threw back his head and laughed. "You *are* good! That has to be the best assessment of me anyone has ever nailed."

She tucked her free hand just inside the waistband of his jeans. "I want more."

"I'll give you more. Whatever you want."

Kennedy sighed. Obviously they were going to do this the hard way. "Brothers or sisters?"

"Only child."

"Parents still living?"

"Mother only. Father dead."

"And you grew up where?"

"Everywhere. My father was in the military."

Now they were getting someplace. "A pilot?"

"Points for the lady. Next question."

"You started down that same path, too, yet one day you quit. You decided you didn't want to turn out the same as your father. Instead of moving from posting to posting, you settled here. But because your family always moved, no place ever felt permanent and you still feel that way. You don't collect things or people."

He shifted restlessly. "While you collect both. I should check on dinner."

She must have touched a nerve if he was that quick to deflect back to her. "I've always thought of it as collecting memories."

"I have memories."

"Sure. Except tomorrow you could toss a few things in a suitcase and move on."

"Couldn't you?"

She dodged the question. "Your father married your mother when they were really young. You didn't repeat that pattern."

"Now you're reaching."

"But I'm betting you long for roots and a big family."

"Why would you say that?"

"It's human nature to hanker after what we don't have. Everyone else's grass always looks greener."

"How did you get so know-it-all?"

"Family trait." She pulled him close. "Will dinner spoil if we don't get to it this second?"

"Not at all. What did you have in mind?"

"A special type of appetizer."

Amused, Sam let Kennedy take the lead. She wanted it, she was accustomed to it; sooner or later she'd get her way, so they might as well settle on that now. Besides, if she wasn't trying so hard to wrestle him for control, he could sit back and learn a lot more by simply observing.

As he expected, she led him to the bedroom; another place she was clearly used to taking the lead. With a shrug and a slither her dress landed in a tiny puddle at her feet. She stepped out of it and stood before him clad only in a black bustier and thong.

He regarded her from behind half-closed lids, then tumbled them down onto the king-size bed.

He sprawled atop her, manacling her wrists above her head with one hand while his other made a lazy assessment of her body. Beneath the bustier her breasts were soft, definitely real. Her waist indented naturally, not requiring the confining lingerie to emphasize her hourglass figure.

She was lush and womanly, but the biggest turn-on of all

was her utter and total confidence—the way she acted like she truly believed there wasn't a man she couldn't have. Yet somewhere, down deep, was the Kennedy he really wanted to get to know. No one could be so confident right down to the core.

He also believed that if he just caved in to her tactics like every other man before him, she'd become bored in a millisecond. Right now she was intrigued, and he had every intention of keeping it that way.

He rubbed his rough cheek against her soft one, inhaled the delicious smell and texture of her hair and her skin. Desire raced through his bloodstream and he worked hard to subdue it.

"You have a body created for sex," he said, working his way from her cheek to her chin to her creamy shoulders and delectable cleavage. "You drive every man mad who sees you."

"Have I been driving you mad?" she asked sweetly.

"You've been keeping me awake at night for years, swollen with desire."

She gave a self-satisfied smile. "How lucky that we reconnected. I'd hate to be the cause of your sleeplessness forever."

Her hips undulated beneath him as she spoke. He still had hold of her hands so she couldn't touch him, but her body rubbed his in a sleekly satisfied way, confident of his state of arousal. If she was a cat, she'd be purring while she rubbed against his hard-on.

Abruptly he released her and rolled off. "Come on," he said. "Let's go eat."

Her reaction was comical. Her mouth dropped open and her eyes narrowed with confusion. "You would rather go eat dinner?"

"No, doll. I would prefer to savor the anticipation. I'm thinking dessert rather than main course."

He scooped up her dress and tugged it over her head.

"Can't we have both?"

"I know you like to have your cake and eat it too, but I promise to make it worth the wait."

She followed him out to the kitchen and watched him dish up their meal—seafood curry on sweet, purple Thai rice. "Are you gay?"

"Most definitely heterosexual."

"Because you cook, and you're neat, and now you're turning down sex. Those all scream 'gay' to me."

"There's a lot more you need to learn about men, Kennedy." He rummaged through the wine fridge and pulled out a dry Reisling. "This should go nicely with the curry."

"I don't think so."

He deliberately pretended to misunderstand her. "Trust me, I know my wine."

"And I know men." He loved that she still had that all-knowing confident smile. What a firecracker!

He smiled back. "Some men. Not all."

"Men are simple creatures."

"Can't argue with you there."

She watched him closely. "But I must admit, I do enjoy a challenge."

He leaned across the table and playfully tweaked the tip of her nose. "Oh, you'll find me that."

He could almost see the wheels of her mind spinning as they ate.

"You know earlier, when you said you thought I was up to something? You were right, in a way. And since you're so perceptive, I'm going to fill you in. But you can't tell my friends."

"I'm listening."

"Justine and Lisa are both just out of bad relationships, and I wanted them to cut loose and have some fun. So I created this sexual scavenger hunt for the three of us."

"Very innovative," he said. "I see why you're so good at your job."

"So you see," Kennedy said, heaving a theatrical sigh, "if you won't sleep with me, I have to move on and find someone who will. I have no intention of coming in last."

"So who's scoring this contest?"

"Miles is keeping track."

"Does Miles get to watch?"

"Of course not. It's based on the honor system."

"How do you know the others won't lie to save face?"

"It's not their way. Besides, this gives them the excuse to behave in ways outside their norm."

Sam leaned forward, intrigued in spite of himself. "So you have to have sex. What else?"

"I need a photo of your cock. Erect would be best."

"Miles will enjoy that part of it."

She grinned. "He deserves some perks."

"What else?"

"A snip of your chest hair. Someone doing a shooter from my navel. I was planning to snag a pair of your boxers the other day when you were in the shower, but you weren't wearing any."

"Problematic," Sam agreed. He was pleased to see she enjoyed her meal. A woman of all appetites. "Can I offer you seconds?"

She blotted her lips with her napkin. "That was delicious, but no, thank you. I'm saving myself for that dessert you promised me."

He pushed back from the table and cleared their dishes. "So if I want to spend more time with you while you're here, you're planning to lead me around with a checklist. Is that how you see it?"

She leaned across the table, pushing her breasts to the forefront. "It'll be fun. I promise."

Sam shook his head. "I'm afraid you'll need to find yourself another boy."

"What?" Her eyes widened in disbelief.

He shrugged and began to load the dishes into the dishwasher. "It's a cute game, I'll give you that. The problem is, I don't play games."

She was at his side in a second, winding her arms around him from behind and rubbing that luscious body up against his. "I let you talk me into Frisbee golf."

He turned to face her, admiring the way she didn't lose her hold. "What kind of man would I be if I just went along with what you're proposing?"

"A sporting one?" she said, her lips parted provocatively.

"You won't respect me in the morning."

"Oh, but I will. If you're half as good as I bet you are."

How hard-to-get did he want to play? "Since you put it that way, I would hate to have it said Sam Watson is a poor sport."

Hands beneath her ass, he lifted her clear off her feet and slid her onto the kitchen counter, pushing up her dress as he did so. He reached under her dress and ripped off her underwear.

"Ooh," Kennedy breathed. "I love it when you take over."

"Just you wait."

She wrapped her legs around his waist for balance. He plunged his hands through her hair and plundered her lips. They were soft and sweet and hot all at the same time.

He'd known once he kissed her that there would be no going back. No pretending he didn't want her with a burning need in his gut.

He swiftly got rid of the dress, then played with her breasts through the bustier, teasing the cresting nipples where they peaked over the lace, egging him on by playing hide-and-seek, till that too was discarded. "You're magnificent!"

He took a step back to admire her fully: shapely legs, rounded hips, nipped-in waist, and voluptuous breasts. Then he picked her up and carried her onto the deck where the hot tub hummed in its darkened nook. He put her down, removed the tub's lid, and started on his own clothes. By the time he'd stripped she was already relaxing in the water.

"I had a feeling water sex was on the list."

"So intuitive," she said.

With a touch of the controls he activated the jets. The underwater lighting changed colors: first red, then green, then aqua and lavender.

He reached down and captured one of her feet for a massage. He ran his fingers between her toes, probing sensitive nerves and tendons from her heel to her ankle.

"Mmm," she said with her head back. "That feels wonderful."

He attended the other foot, then pulled her forward so she straddled him. Her breasts bobbed enticingly on the surface of the water and he fondled their fullness.

She shifted so that her clit was pressed to his swollen cock, giving a little wiggle of pleasure. Her hands got into the act, exploring the planes of his chest against hers. "I like your hot tub."

Wisps of baby-fine hair at her hairline started to curl in the steam engulfing them.

"And here I thought you were interested in me for one thing only."

"I have a *very* long list for the sexcapades hunt."

"Right—I'll be right back."

He climbed out and went inside, then returned with a bottle of cognac. "One belly button shooter coming up. Sit up on the side, then lean back." He poured some of the fiery liquid into her navel, then leaned down and lapped it up.

She giggled. "That's cold. And it tickles."

"Allow me to warm it for you."

He splashed more cognac onto her breasts, then licked them very clean, tugging each turgid nipple into his mouth and sucking hard, rewarded by the instant hardening, the rise in her breathing, the tensing of her muscles as her desire built to match his.

He eased her back and, eyes intent on hers, drizzled cognac onto her magic triangle.

"That's very wasteful if you don't plan to drink it."

"Don't you worry. I have no intention of spilling a drop."

He tongued her softly and heard her responding moan. A heady combination of fiery cognac and equally hot woman filled his mouth, and desire bolted through his system. He got it under control and concentrated on Kennedy; her special scent and taste underlying the liquor. Petal-soft lips gave way to the stamen of the inner flower.

He barely grazed it with his tongue, felt a quivering response, then pulled back to concentrate on her inner thighs, tonguing and licking and sampling their softness as she tried to direct him back to her heated core.

"You've kept me waiting a long time, Sam Watson. I'm not used to waiting."

He sipped the impatience from her lips, sharing her taste and the cognac as he played with her breasts. "Patience, my lovely."

He continued to kiss and fondle her, amused and intrigued by the way she angled herself against his thigh, rubbing her heated opening on his leg, her breath rising and falling in needy panting gasps, until he felt it. Her back arched, her muscles tensed; she gasped softly into him, and climaxed.

He caught and held her, feeling the tension slowly seep from every particle of her. Gradually her heavy breathing slowed, then her eyes fluttered open. "Lord, I needed that."

"And to think," Sam said, "we're just getting started."

Chapter Seven

$\mathcal{N}$ever before had any man made Kennedy come simply by kissing her while she rubbed against him. Delicious! A little shivery aftershock rippled through her as she slowly slid back into the swirling water. Its soothing warmth enfolded her, enhancing the lingering tingles of her orgasm.

"You are a man of many talents!"

He settled next to her and pulled her onto his lap. "You really couldn't wait, could you?"

"Think of it as a warm-up—like stretching before a work-out."

Sam smiled a slow, confident smile that did funny squirmy things to her insides. "I like that."

She reached down and played with his cock, tickling his balls. She palmed him slowly, avoiding the sensitive tip. "Let's just get one thing clear."

"What's that?"

She angled his erection so she could enjoy the slow glide of him against her clit. "Don't you dare come as quickly as I did."

"I promise."

She felt him throbbing and pulsing. She was hot and wet and aching to feel him inside, but she needed to make him frantic for her, burn for her until he couldn't see straight.

She tweaked his nipples with her fingertips, caressed his chest and shoulders as she bobbed slightly, pleasuring them both without actual penetration. "Tell me what you like."

"I like the way you feel against me. I like the way you're not afraid to try new things. I like the way you know who you are and what you want, with no qualms about going after it."

"Qualms are for pussies." She tangled her fingers through his hair, her nails raking his scalp, then leaned down and took his nipple in her mouth, sucking first, then taking a light nip. She dragged her nails across his back hard enough so he'd feel them, but not hard enough to mark his skin. "I want you inside."

"I figured that."

"But first I want to suck you."

"I thought you'd never ask."

He stood, his cock jutting proudly between them. She rained the lightest of butterfly kisses over, under, and around, and felt him swell even larger, followed by his satisfying groan of pleasure. He set the pace as she tongued, then sucked, before giving him her trademark whirl across the tip.

She knew she'd hit her mark when he pulled out abruptly, his breath whistling between his teeth while his entire body trembled. She smiled, stood, and leaned over the edge of the tub, waggling her tush. "I like it doggy-style."

His hands caressed her behind while she reached between them and guided him toward her.

"Just a sec." He reached for a condom and she couldn't believe how fast he got it open and in place. "Ready?"

"More than ready."

He entered her with a delicious fullness, and she sighed aloud in pleasure—especially when he reached around to play with her clit, which all but jumped up to welcome him. Her orgasm rocked through her before he was all the way in. Full penetration brought a second. Followed by a third.

He stopped moving. "I can feel you squeezing me."

"Like this?" She tightened her inner muscles.

"Just like that." He stayed completely still inside her while she played him, squeezing and releasing, adding her own special pivot: side to side, then up and down.

He reached around to palm her breasts, nibbling the back of her neck as she made soft noises of approval, her body cleaving to his, liquid and responsive. Totally open to absorb the pleasure of their joining, she matched each thrust as Sam accelerated the pace.

Water splashed around them as he drove himself into her, adding to the noise as Kennedy shrieked and thrashed and clung to the side of the tub. Orgasm spiraled atop orgasm until, finally, he gave a triumphant yell and emptied himself into her.

Lisa was the first one home from her date. She joined Miles for a nightcap and tried unsuccessfully to pump him for information on the contest. "I can't believe everyone is being so closemouthed," she complained. "Usually you can't shut any of us up."

"It's not polite to kiss and tell," Miles said.

"We're telling you," she pointed out.

"And your secrets are safe with me, girlfriend." He flashed her a smug look. "You seem a pretty lively trio."

"I was dull when I was married. Maybe that's why he strayed."

Miles slanted her a quelling look. "There is no excuse for playing around."

"Miles, I didn't have you pegged for such an old-fashioned guy."

"Who's an old-fashioned guy?" Justine entered just then. "Not your date, I hope."

"Miles was just telling me that he believes in monogamy."

Justine's euphoric glow faded instantly. "Good for you, Miles. There should be more like you."

Lisa said, "Justine, Mr. Married fed you a line. He was good, and you believed him."

"Because I wanted to," Justine said. "Same as you

believed Les till you caught him in the act." She bit her lip. "Sorry. That was bitchy."

Lisa's voice was low. "Sometimes it's easier to believe someone's lies than face the truth."

"'Specially when they're telling you what you want to hear. What's a girl need to do to get a drink around this place?" Justine asked Miles.

Miles jumped up to make it just as Kennedy waltzed in the door. "Evening, ladies. Are we all having fun yet?"

"Where did your date take *you*?" Lisa blurted out. She'd never seen Kennedy with a hair out of place before, let alone disheveled and not seeming to care.

"We played Frisbee golf."

"*You?*" Justine said.

"I kid you not." Kennedy took a sip from the icy martini Miles presented to her. "What about you two?"

"Boating," Justine said. "Skinny-dipping, too. Oops!" She slapped a hand across her mouth.

"I'm thinking water sex," Kennedy said with a grin. "Lisa?"

"We were mostly getting to know each other. He showed me his golf trophies."

"Ho, ho. Is that anything like showing you his etchings?"

"Richard isn't like that," Lisa said. "He's very sincere."

Kennedy wagged a finger. "No falling for the first guy you go out with. You know better."

"I'm hitting the hot tub before bed," Justine said. "Anyone else?"

"I've had my fill of the hot tub tonight," Kennedy said with a lecherous wink.

"Count me out, too." Lisa settled on the couch with her drink.

"And I'm going to say good night, ladies." Miles took his leave and Justine headed for the hot tub, leaving Lisa and Kennedy alone.

"What's up?" Kennedy said. "Spill."

"Why does something have to be up?" Lisa wished she didn't always feel so defensive around Kennedy. Much as she admired her friend's zest for life, she did mind that her own seemed dull in comparison.

"I know you, darlin'. You like this guy."

"I do," Lisa said. "He's sweet and sincere."

"And the problem is?"

"Richard reminds me a lot of Les."

"That doesn't sound good. In what way is he like Les?"

"The golden boy, the charmed life. He had the dream, the drive to succeed, and he made it as a golf pro. Whether it was effortless or not, he made it seem that way."

"Why did he stop?"

"His wife didn't like his lifestyle."

"Are you saying he quit for her?"

"No, that makes him sound weak when he's not. At the top of his game, he evaluated the lifestyle and decided family life was more important. So he bowed out, and found he didn't really miss it."

"Right choice, wrong reasons?" Kennedy said.

"I guess. Unfortunately his wife still wasn't content, and nowhere near as determined as he was to make the marriage work. When he found her fooling around on him, he ended it."

"You two have a lot in common."

"Too much," Lisa said. "He feels like the yang to my yin. We're just so connected, and how is that even possible? I don't *want* that connection," she wailed.

"Honey, deep down, we all want that connection."

"Even you?"

Kennedy laughed. "As incredible as it may seem I too am looking for something I haven't found yet."

Lisa blinked and sat forward. "I thought you flitted from man to man just because you can, because you're so good at it."

"Everyone thinks that. Don't get me wrong; I enjoy it. But just because I haven't met anyone I want to have an exclusive with, doesn't mean I'm opposed to the concept."

"Do you think we wind up being like our parents, no matter what?"

Kennedy's laughter faded abruptly. "God, I hope not."

"Sorry." Lisa sighed. She'd forgotten that Kennedy had some serious "Mommy Dearest" issues. Kennedy always said she was more comfortable around men than women because she'd been raised by her father.

"How did it wind up being just you and your dad, anyway?"

"Some women just aren't cut out to be mothers."

"Ever think about having a baby yourself?"

Kennedy gave her head a dismissive shake. "I'll leave that to you and Justine with your maternal instincts."

"Who's got maternal instincts?" Justine arrived in time to catch the end of the conversation.

"Not me," Kennedy said, rising. "We're here to have fun—not get all serious."

Lisa sat forward. "Speaking of fun, have you heard about the Grand Gala this weekend? Richard said it's the bash of the year, with celebs flying in from all over. Think there's any chance we might score tickets?"

"What? Richard didn't invite you?" Kennedy teased.

Lisa lobbed a pillow at her. "Like he'd have an extra ticket lying around."

"Anything's possible. Let's ask our all-knowing Miles what he knows about it." Kennedy stretched and yawned. "Goodness, I'm not used to so much fresh air. I'm off to find my pillow."

Upstairs, Kennedy gave herself a high five in the mirror as she brushed her teeth. Things were proceeding exactly according to plan.

Sam watched approvingly as his golf ball arched high and landed on the green. "I'm only telling you guys this because you both like the Seattle babes, and you need to know what they're up to."

Eric took his shot. "Aren't they here on vacation?"

Richard's ball bounced onto the green to join the other two. "I told Lisa about the Grand Gala, then I felt bad for not inviting her."

"You can't invite her and leave out the other two. Eric and I have our evening planned," Sam added.

"To some degree," Eric said. "What *are* they up to?"

"Kennedy dreamed up some wacky sexual scavenger hunt. The girls are running back to Miles with every juicy detail, and the poor bastard is keeping score."

Richard laughed so hard, he blew his putt. "I've never been used as a sex object before, but I'm definitely not opposed to the concept."

"Is Kennedy as wild as she comes across?"

"Like a big cat out in the jungle." Sam made his putt, watching with satisfaction as the ball ringed the cup and dropped in. If only it was this easy to corral Kennedy!

Lisa

Sexcapades

I'm on the board, finally!

collect:

— your date's boxers

✓ his favorite golf glove

— a snip of his chest hair

score:

— a shooter he slurps from your belly button

— an extravagant piece of jewelry

— a picture of his penis

enjoy:

— sex in a limo

— water sex (indoors or out)

— sex outdoors (double points for daytime)

— skinny-dipping with your date

— dress-up sex

— him as your slave, bondage included

Chapter Eight

Lisa stared fretfully at her silent cell phone. She knew Richard had to be busy between his book and his work and the upcoming Grand Gala; he'd call when he got time. Still . . . She drummed her fingers impatiently.

Her actions didn't go unnoticed by her friends as they lazed around the pool, happily waited on by Miles. Kennedy had decreed they deserved a do-nothing day to rest up before going out on the prowl later.

Kennedy reached across, grabbed Lisa's phone, and shut it off.

"Hey!" Lisa yelped. "Give that back!"

"You ever hear of a watched pot not boiling?" Kennedy teased.

Lisa slumped back on her padded lounger and straightened her sun hat. "I thought he was different from the others."

"It's high time you learned they're all the same. Take the sex and run." Kennedy smiled her Cheshire cat smile. "Fortunately, two can play at that game, and there's plenty more where he came from. Walker Hook is a man-mecca."

Lisa pounded her fist against her thigh. "What's wrong with me that I take men at face value? I got blindsided by Les; now Richard." She almost leapt out of her seat at the sound of the doorbell, her heart giving a ridiculous surge of hope.

"Sit still," Kennedy hissed. "Miles will get it."

Lisa glanced over at Justine, asleep on her stomach, her dark head pillowed in her arms. Why couldn't she be more like that?

"I take back what I said last night. All that hooey about yin and yang and connections."

"There's plenty more men out there. We just have to go find them."

Justine rolled over and smothered a yawn. "I'm ready." She looked up as Miles approached. "Who was at the door?"

"Someone very special." Before any of them could ask more, Miles took a bow. "Rumor has it you girls were keen to attend the Grand Gala for S.C.S., so I made it my mission to secure you tickets."

Kennedy clapped her hands in delight. "It was sold out months ago. How did you manage that?"

Miles gave a self-satisfied smile. "Let's just say I have my sources."

"The Grand Gala!" Lisa echoed. Richard would be there. "I have nothing to wear."

"The Mighty Miles has that covered as well. A friend of mine is an up-and-coming designer. Tomorrow I'll take you to his place, where I'm certain you'll find something dynamite."

"Speaking of shopping . . ." Kennedy said. "It's nearly time we went shopping for men."

The golf course lounge was full, but in typical fashion, Kennedy managed to secure prime seats at the bar, an excellent vantage point to see and be seen.

Lisa didn't look far before she spun around. "It's Richard. Maybe he won't see me."

"Yup." Justine made a lazy perusal. "He didn't see you."

Lisa stiffened. "He didn't see me? What is he? Blind?"

"He looks actually quite busy," Kennedy offered.

Lisa snuck a quick glance, then wished she hadn't, for Richard was with a woman, their heads close together in an intense conversation.

"I guess I owe him a big thank-you for getting me out into the dating pool again."

Justine shrugged blithely. "Look around you, my friend. So many men, so little time."

So few who interest me, Lisa thought.

Kennedy leaned around Justine to face Lisa. "The guy truly did you a favor. You told me you were afraid he was a repeat of Les, and the fact that he's with another woman means you're absolutely correct. So get out there and find someone the polar opposite of both of them."

"Good advice." Lisa downed her drink in a single swallow, pushed herself off her bar stool, and made her way across the room to a Mr. Tall, Dark, and Handsome who stood with his back to her. Boldly, she tapped him on the shoulder. He turned.

With bravado, Lisa looked him up and down. "Don't I know you from somewhere?"

His coffee-dark eyes lingered on hers. "If not, I'm quite certain we can rectify that."

They smiled at each other, and Lisa took a breath. "Isn't this where you ask if you can buy me a drink?"

"Darling . . ." Behind her, Miles pushed her hair aside and whispered into her ear, "Your gay-dar's off, hon. This one's mine."

"Oh." She glanced from Miles to his friend. "Sorry."

His friend smiled a million megawatt smile. "No harm done. I also enjoy the company of women."

"Trust me, it's not company she's on the hunt for," Miles said.

"Miles is right." Lisa sighed. "Not only am I in last place, I deserve to lose points for this fumble."

"It's not whether you win or lose, silly girl, it's all in how you play the game."

"Apparently I'm not playing terribly well," Lisa muttered. "Well, I'd best get back to my friends."

"Don't forget. Frock shopping tomorrow," Miles sang out as Lisa returned to her seat.

"That advice sucked," she said to Justine. "I pick out the type I never normally go for, only to find out he's gay."

Kennedy laughed. "At least there's a good reason you don't usually go for that type. But you did catch the attention of your golf pro."

"Perfect." Lisa sighed, swirling her new drink. "Why not have the entire room witness my humiliation?"

She saw the way her two friends exchanged looks. "Stop talking about me with your eyes!"

Kennedy shook her head. "Throw the storybook away, Lisa. There is no Prince Charming on a white charger coming to sweep you off your feet. He doesn't exist."

Lisa deflated. "But Richard seemed so sincere."

"I'm sure he was, at the time. That was then, this is now." Kennedy tossed back the rest of her drink. "Let's move along."

Lisa slid off her stool. "You two go ahead. I'm going back to the villa."

"It's too early," Justine protested.

"Not to me."

Despite her friends' protests, Lisa parted from them outside.

"At least grab a cab," Justine said.

"I feel like fresh air. The walk will do me good." She gave them both a quick hug. "Go have fun. I'll snap out of my funk by tomorrow, I promise."

Lisa window-shopped her way back. Would life be any different if Les hadn't died on the ski hill? Probably not. Even though they'd been working on a reconciliation, the damage had been done, the myth of happily ever after shattered.

The villa was dark and silent, just what she needed after the noisy bar. Impulsively, she donned a robe and went out onto the pool deck to view the stars. Maybe they held some answers.

The water shimmered in the moonlight, beckoning her till she shed her robe and dove into the deep end. The water felt divine. Surely this counted as skinny-dipping? Even though the implication was that one wouldn't be alone for the deed. She surfaced and rolled over, floating on her back and staring skyward. What a gorgeous, clear night. No clouds, just hundreds of glittering stars surrounding the moon.

She rolled over and struck out at a brisk crawl, hoping to tire herself out enough to sleep.

But she hadn't swum for long before she felt herself start to lag. *It must be those martinis. They're energy sappers.*

She paused to tread water and catch her breath . . . and saw Richard standing at the far end, like something she'd conjured up. She blinked but he didn't disappear.

"How's the water?" he asked.

"Why don't you come find out?" She tossed her head, excitement roaring through her. Was this her, naked in a pool at night, the stars and moon the only witness as she invited a man to join her?

Richard didn't need much coaxing to shed his clothes and dive in. The underwater lights charted his progress toward her before he bobbed to the surface in front of her.

"How did you get in here?"

"If I confess to jumping the fence, will you have me arrested for trespassing?"

"That all depends." She could see droplets of water on his long, thick lashes, framing her reflection in his eyes. The new Lisa—daring, bold, and fun.

"Challenge you to a race?"

"I don't want to race." He clasped her around the waist, using his feet to keep them afloat as he maneuvered to the side of the pool. "I've been intending to call you."

Lisa gave a careless shrug. "I was busy."

"So I noticed earlier."

"So were you," she couldn't resist adding.

"That was my agent."

"Your agent?"

"I told you about the book. She's working with my publicist, mapping out a strategy. A tour and signings, things I'd rather not bother with, but which she assures me are necessary for a successful launch."

"Like being on a pro tour, only different."

"Maybe that's the problem. I feel like I've done all this before."

"Perhaps you'll make it up Seattle way at some point."

"Book signing or not, I expect I will." He moved in as he spoke and she was ready, lips parted, pulse clamoring, senses atingle.

She sighed into him as he kissed her, her hands atop his shoulders for balance. He lifted her legs and wrapped them around his waist.

"That's better." He spoke against her lips while his chest got reacquainted with her breasts.

"Much better," she agreed, angling his head to hers as *she* kissed *him*. The first kiss had been a greeting. The second one was deep and hungry, demanding fulfillment, and excitement spiraled through her as his need met and matched hers.

She raked her nails through his hair to his scalp, then trailed her hands down the back of his neck, over his shoulders to his chest, where she ruffled the thatch of hair teasing her breasts. Ankles locked behind him, she pivoted in his embrace, making certain he could feel the heat radiating from her V Zone.

He groaned and ran his hands up the slope of her spine to her shoulder blades, then back down in a slow glide to cradle her behind and lever her tight against him.

She loosened her grip and guided his hands to where her breasts bobbed pertly between them, peeking from the surface of the water, alabaster white in the moonlight, shadowed by the areola of her nipples. She moaned softly as he palmed them, her nipples hardening into tight buds of temptation.

He ducked his head and obligingly sucked first one, then the other, then both together. A bolt of sensation shot through her directly from her breasts to her inner core, and she shivered, purring her pleasure.

"I need to taste all of you." He maneuvered their entwined bodies to the shallow end and positioned her on the edge, her feet and ankles in the warm water. When he knelt on the steps before her, she leaned back using her hands for balance. Her legs parted, liquid beneath his touch.

He moved to the inside of one knee, licking and tonguing his way slowly toward her, stopping just shy of his target before he repeated the procedure on her other leg. Tingles ran up the backs of her legs from her knees to her upper thigh. She could feel the tiny rosebud of her clitoris blossom in anticipation.

His heated breath on her outer lips was followed by the resultant swell of blood rushing to turn up the heat inside and out.

Her inner lips and clit throbbed with need, impatient to have him seek their sweetness. But he detoured back to her soft inner thigh, then up to ring her navel. Finally his mouth slid over her mound to give her the most intimate kiss of all.

He used his hands to gently open her, granting himself better access till she decided to help and leave his hands free for other things, like her breasts.

First he laved her hardening clit, then gently sucked it. She caught her breath and reared up in pleasure as his tongue penetrated her inner sanctum with a lashing possession.

Planting her feet on the step for leverage, she moved with him and against him, rode him into ecstasy as the floodgates of fulfillment opened wide and she sobbed out her pleasure.

He stayed with her, nuzzled her inner thigh and held her gently while the aftershocks subsided and her breathing matched the ragged rise and fall of his.

Then he scooped her in his arms and carried her to a nearby lounge.

She opened her arms in welcome. "It's about time you made love to me."

He loomed above her, legs planted apart, face in shadow—
her conquering hero. The moonlight played with the silhouette of her proud, bold lord, accentuating his maleness. God,
she was doing it again, lost in the fantasy fairy tale. *It's about
the sex,* she reminded herself. And a chance to beat her friends
at their game.

What is he waiting for?

"You're like a goddess in the moonlight. A gift from the
heavens."

She reached out, clamped his erect cock, and drew him
to her waiting lips.

He pulsed against her as she slid her hand from tip to root,
taking his measure, murmuring her approval. He felt hot and
ready, the bold pulse of engorged blood filling him beneath her
palm. She blew on him, pressed a kiss to the tip, then circled
him with her tongue: light, teasing twirls that brought a groan
to his lips and a tiny pearl of moisture to the tip.

She made a ring of her thumb and forefinger and slid it
slowly, lovingly down his length and back, feeling the silky
glide of skin beneath her touch. Hearing the hiss of his indrawn breath, she reveled in her power as he widened his
stance and slid his hands through her hair, inviting her to
taste him fully.

She parted her lips and admitted him entrance, unable to
accommodate his full length. Still, she did her best, using one
hand to caress his balls and the other hand to find the sweet
spot just beyond his testicles. She knew she'd found it when
he jumped and swore softly, and gently removed himself
from her torturing tongue and lips.

"Something wrong?" she asked wickedly, enjoying her ability to drive him crazy.

"It's time for the main event." He pulled her atop him, to straddle him.

Hands on his chest for balance, she dragged her hot and hungry pleasure palace up and down the throbbing length of his erect cock, dampening them both with the dew of her desire, rubbing his tip against her clit while her breasts bobbed in his face and he caught them in his mouth.

"Oh!" Waves of sensation flooded her in a sudden rush of pleasure. She hadn't known she could come again before he was even inside her, so her orgasm caught her unawares.

She glanced down to see him watching her with an intensity that sent a sizzle through her. Maybe she hadn't imagined their special connection earlier.

Eyes locked with his, she slowly positioned him at her entranceway, then gloved the softest hardness imaginable with her welcoming warmth.

She exhaled sharply in pleasure at the absolute perfection of the way he fit and filled her. She straightened, lifted her hair off the back of her neck, then let it fall, her skin savoring the sensual swish of its release before she arched her back and rested her hands on his knees, feeling and finding new sensations each time she shifted her pose.

Never had she felt such freedom to explore her own sexuality. In the past her anxieties had held her back, focused on making sure her partner was well-pleasured. This time it was all about her and the freedom Richard provided. Heady stuff. She pivoted forward and back, side to side, riding him first fast, then slow. Mini eruptions exploded one after the other and she absorbed each and every one of them, a pleasure point unto themselves. What had passed for an orgasm in the past was now only a prelude.

"Turn around," Richard said. "I want to admire your ass."

Obliging she spun around, presenting him with her backside to fondle as she discovered a whole new angle of entry. "This is good," she said. "Very good."

His balls were hitting her clit with a delightful pressure that became even more intense when she palmed his balls and touched herself at the same time, riding hard.

Mini orgasms spiraled into a full-force climax. She felt her insides shatter, robbing her of conscious thought, then the force of his release hurtled her over the top of beyond.

Kennedy

Sexcapades

collect:

___ your date's boxers — *problematic*

✓ his favorite golf glove

✓ a snip of his chest hair

score:

✓ a shooter he slurps from your belly button

___ an extravagant piece of jewelry

✓ a picture of his penis

enjoy:

___ sex in a limo

✓ water sex (indoors or out)

___ sex outdoors (double points for daytime) *Hot tub?*

___ skinny-dipping with your date

___ dress-up sex

___ him as your slave, bondage included

___ *Meet his mother*

Chapter Nine

"That bar was a bust," Kennedy said as she followed Justine from the cab to the villa.

Justine unlocked the door. "You claim you never get emotionally attached to the men you sleep with. How is that possible?"

Kennedy grinned. "Years of practice."

"It seems very guy-like. Yet both of us have come home alone."

"None of those guys tonight did anything for me."

"Me either," Justine said, a little too quickly.

Kennedy tossed her a searching look. "I'd advise against getting attached to Eric. Or is it too late?"

Justine gave a helpless shrug. "It started out as the perfect zipless fuck."

"Try not kissing on the lips."

"I like to kiss."

"Apparently you're not the only one." Catching sight of movement through the windows, Kennedy lowered her voice and tugged at Justine's hand to get her attention. She pointed through the darkened living room to the heavily shadowed pool deck, where moonlight bathed the contours of a man and a woman on the double chaise longue, their limbs twined together.

"Who would have guessed?" Kennedy said drily.

Justine nodded. "Lisa's home bagging points while we're out turning down offers, " she whispered.

Kennedy headed into the kitchen, Justine on her heels. "What's wrong with this picture?" she muttered.

"That was Richard she was with, right?" Justine said.

"Honey, they all look the same in the dark. I wonder if Miles left us snacks." She opened the fridge. "Bless his heart." She set the tray of canapes on the counter and pulled off the plastic covering while Justine moved toward the wine rack.

"What do you want to drink?"

"It feels like a Shiraz kind of evening."

"Shiraz it is."

Kennedy watched Justine open the bottle of wine. "This trip certainly has been good therapy for Lisa," Kennedy said.

Justine grinned. "Better than retail therapy any day."

Lisa floated in on the end of their conversation, belting her robe. "What's better than retail therapy?"

"That happy little just-got-laid glow you're wearing," Justine said.

Lisa flushed. "Richard, um, managed to surprise me."

"So it would appear. Where is his studlyness?"

"He has a really early day tomorrow. Besides, I don't think I'm ready to spend the night with him. That's a whole other level of intimacy."

"Mr. Married never could spend the night. I would have loved to wake up in his arms, just once," Justine said.

"Well, I'm with Lisa," Kennedy said. "Use them for sex and send them on their way."

"Yet you're both here alone," Lisa pointed out.

"We were just discussing that very thing," Justine said. "Remember when we all first met?"

"Sure, the golf lesson," Lisa said.

"And you and I started chatting about business. How between your gallery and my designing we could help each other. Kennedy only talked to the pro. It was like we weren't even there."

"That's right." Lisa glanced at Kennedy. "We didn't like you very much."

"Thanks." Kennedy tried to laugh off the sting of Lisa's words, knowing her friend was only being honest. Having never had women friends before, Kennedy had been like an infant learning to walk, figuring out it was okay to accept friendship, and how to be a friend in return. It was a lesson she was still learning.

"I blame my mother. In all those beauty shows and talent contests she put me in, the other girl was always the enemy. You sure didn't make friends." She shrugged. "You know the rest."

She'd learned long ago to talk about it as if it didn't matter. When she failed to win every single contest and competition, her mother unceremoniously dumped her with her father. Mommy Dearest dropped from sight and Kennedy learned not to trust women. Particularly the ones who pretended to care about her in order to get close to her father. It was far easier to put her trust in men, starting with her father's friends, who were always nice to her. They helped her understand a man's mind-set and how to use it to her advantage.

Something she was still doing today.

"Come on, girls. Let's go! Chop, chop!" Miles paced the front entrance hall and clapped his hands for emphasis. "Your chariot awaits."

"Our pumpkin, you mean," Justine teased. "Don't look at me like that. I'm on time."

"We're all on time," Kennedy said, coming down the stairs with Lisa behind her. "You're just impatient. You'd think you were the one going frock shopping."

"Darlings, I'm living vicariously through you three."

"And you get to see your boyfriend," Kennedy said as they piled in the Jag, Miles behind the wheel.

"No, my sweet, I get to see the transformation firsthand." He pursed his lips theatrically. "And I have a little surprise for you afterward."

"A surprise? What kind of surprise?"

But despite their pleas, Miles remained tight-lipped as they drove to the designer's studio and showroom.

This was Kennedy's kind of shopping. Miles rang the bell, gave his name through the intercom, and the unmarked door swung open. Inside, they were met by three personal shoppers. Down a corridor and through a second doorway, the girls found themselves inside a vast warehouse where the first stop was the bar for a glass of sparkling wine.

"Have fun, ladies." Miles settled himself into a comfy leather chair with a men's fashion magazine and a latte.

"When do we get to meet your buddy?" Kennedy asked.

"He'll pop by later."

Justine rubbed her hands together in glee. "I don't know where to start."

"That's where I come in," said her shopper, a serious-looking girl with glasses and buzzed hair.

"Lead on," Justine said happily, raising her glass in a toast.

Lisa obediently followed her shopper, leaving Kennedy with a far-too-attractive young woman named Theresa, whose eyes swept over her from head to toe. Kennedy held her ground and stared back, eyes narrowed. Theresa's hair was too glossy black to be natural, and with that translucent white skin and red lips, she looked like Snow White.

"Something for the Gala, correct? I suggest we start over here." Theresa strode ahead wheeling an empty wardrobe rack, not even looking back to make sure Kennedy was following. Kennedy mentally took her outfit apart, piece by piece. How could she possibly trust this woman to make her look her absolute best?

"I like black," Kennedy said.

Theresa dismissed her words with a quick shake of her glossy dark head. "Everyone will be wearing black. Black is too safe."

"It's also sexy."

Theresa smiled, revealing perfect white teeth. "There'll be no problem with you looking sexy. It's as natural as breathing."

"Easy for you to say, you're still young," Kennedy retorted.

Theresa sorted through racks of clothing on the sample wall. "In Europe, women are considered more attractive with life experience."

"We're not in Europe. One day, every woman walks into a room and realizes she's no longer the babe. No one's looking at her."

Theresa laughed as she selected gown after gown and hung them on her rack. "It's all in the attitude, and you've got it. Look at Mae West."

"Kill me if I ever have her thighs."

"You have perfect proportions. Our designs won't even need alterations."

Kennedy took a sip of her wine. "What do you recommend?"

"Chocolate is this season's new black. See the way this taffeta catches the light?"

Kennedy fingered the fabric. She loved the smell of new textiles. "It's almost got a purple undertone." The gown was sleeveless, snug through the bodice, rounded over the breasts, and nipped in at the waist before it exploded in layers of skirts and overskirts.

"A very subtle aubergine." Theresa continued to pull gowns from the wall, accepting some, rejecting others till eventually Kennedy found herself in a huge tent-like dressing room with her friends.

"Isn't this fun?" Lisa squealed.

"I guess." Justine looked overwhelmed. *Help,* she silently entreated Kennedy.

"Start with the red," Kennedy suggested.

"For the scarlet woman, you mean?"

"Oh, get off it, Justine. Get changed. Lisa! That's absolutely the one."

"God, I look like a bride." Fair-haired Lisa, in fairyland white with silver sequins, rhinestones, and pearls, twirled, then raced out of the change room. "Miles! What do you think?"

"Now I really feel like a fairy godmother."

"As long as our gowns don't turn into rags at midnight." Kennedy laughed. "Justine, zip me, please?"

"My dear, that frock was made for you," Miles said as Kennedy made her way to the main viewing room, turning this way and that in front of a three-way mirror.

"What about me?" Justine came out in a body-hugging, lipstick-red sheath, dramatic with her dark hair.

"Wow!" The three friends stood eyeing themselves and one another in the mirrors. "We look so different."

"Different from one another, or different from the way we normally look?"

"Both," Kennedy said. Normally she wouldn't have looked twice at her gown, yet it was both elegant and divaish at the same time, and the taffeta's sheen gave her luminescent skin the luster of pearls.

Miles snapped his fingers in the air to the hovering staff. "Quickly ladies: shoes, bags, jewelry. Do it up right. Then we'll go for lunch. Shopping always makes me hungry."

Outside, Miles loaded their booty into the trunk of the car while Justine and Lisa clambered in. Kennedy was about to join them when she paused and reversed her actions.

"I just thought of something I need to do."

"But what about lunch?"

"I'll catch up with you in a bit."

"Don't be long." Miles pouted. "Or you'll ruin my surprise."

Lisa looked at Justine. "What do you think she's up to?"

Justine craned her head till they lost sight of Kennedy. "I don't know, but she's been acting odd."

"How so?"

"Distracted, for lack of a better word. Like sometimes she's here, but she's not really here."

"She's always had her own agenda," Lisa said.

"I have a funny feeling her agenda has recently changed."

"I know she's been worried about work. The agency recently hired a whole slew of new young talent; I was surprised when she was willing to take this week off."

"That's what I mean. Something isn't quite adding up," Justine said.

*   *   *

Kennedy spotted Sam and stopped, pretending to be engrossed in the window display of a nearby shop. She caught sight of his reflection in the window as he stopped behind her and her pulse did a little two-step.

"Funny, you don't strike me as a dog person," Sam said.

Kennedy inwardly flinched. She hadn't even noticed what type of store she'd paused in front of. "What brings you this way?"

"Picking up my tux from the cleaners."

"Ah, the Gala tomorrow," Kennedy said casually. "I suppose you have a date?" She couldn't go with him even if he asked her; it would complicate things to no end.

"You bet," Sam said. "Well, see you around." As he sauntered off, she felt a poof of disappointment. Of course he had a date; what did she expect? She made a quick phone call, then hurried to meet the others at the restaurant.

"What are you up to that's so secret?" Kennedy asked Miles. "Where are you taking us?"

"Patience, my lovely. Let it go."

"Let what go?"

"This penchant you have for always needing control."

"I'm not like that," Kennedy sputtered.

Hoots and jeers issued from Justine and Lisa in the backseat.

Kennedy bit back her defensive retort. They were laughing at her, but in a kind and loving way, not that bitchy competitive way she grew up with. Would she ever recover from that legacy?

She folded her arms across her chest. "Someone has to keep an eye on you jokers."

"Here we are." A long driveway wound through a well-tended and manicured lawn before Miles pulled up in front of a heritage mansion.

"What is Elements?" Kennedy read the discreetly lettered sign beside the double French doors.

"Questions, questions." Miles herded them from the car and into a sleek, if somewhat chilly, front reception area.

"Here they are," he trilled as a beautiful, elegantly dressed blonde appeared.

"Excellent. I'm Olivia. You must be Kennedy. You're Justine, and you have to be Lisa." She identified each of them in turn as she shook hands. "Welcome to Elements."

"Thank you, but we don't know why we're here," Lisa blurted.

"Miles, you naughty boy. Elements is a very exclusive spa," Olivia told them.

"You girls have fun." Miles waggled his fingers in their direction. "I'll pick you up later."

"He's taking this fairy godmother stuff to heart," Kennedy said.

Once they changed into monogrammed robes, the girls were settled into the waiting lounge, a cozy room that was once the parlor of the old mansion, and were served champagne.

"Kennedy?" Olivia didn't so much enter the room, she glided. "If you're ready."

"What sort of treatment did Miles book for me?" she asked.

"I think you'll be very pleased with the arrangements Miles has made." From the elevator, she opened a door and ushered Kennedy into a large cave-like treatment room tiled from floor to ceiling with earth-tone tiles, illuminated by a single lit candle. Its subtle fragrance was exotic, bringing incense to mind.

A huge tiled tub occupied one corner, its surface speckled with floating rose petals of pink, red, and white. The smell of essential oils perfumed the air.

"You can slip out of your robe and onto the massage table. On your back to start with."

Kennedy shrugged out of her robe and hung it on the back of the door. The comfily contoured table hugged her, enclosing her in welcoming, soothing warmth. She'd barely wiggled herself into a comfy hollow when she felt her arms caught and held at a forty-five-degree angle to her body.

"Hey!"

A velvet, dark eye mask, cool and scented, was laid across her eyes. The lower part of the table separated so that her legs were parted, and she heard a muffled click as her ankles were fastened in place.

A fragrant vial was placed beneath her nose. "Take a good long sniff," Olivia said.

"I hope you're not some lesbian friend of Miles who fantasizes about converting a straight girl."

"Not at all, Kennedy. This is about you and control."

"I never lose control." She took a long slow smell of the oil as if to make her point. "I like it. It's relaxing."

"That's the idea."

Seconds later she heard the whoosh of the door closing. As she lay there, wondering what kind of bizarre scheme Miles had cooked up, she heard a second door open and sensed the presence of someone in the room with her.

"You told me you rarely allow yourself to play, Kennedy. Are you game to play?"

"Sam?" Kennedy laughed. "Never let it be said I can't be surprised."

"I have the feeling you'll be great fun to surprise." She felt the light tickling sensation of something downy and feather-like across her skin, starting with her sensitive under-arm and moving slowly from wrist to torso: first one side, then the other.

"That feels good," Kennedy said. "But I'm not in the least bit ticklish."

"You sure?" He trailed the feathery device across her ribs and circled each breast, edging closer and closer to her nip-ples. She felt them pucker and pull tight in anticipation, felt her nether regions swell and moisten.

"You know I'm impatient," Kennedy said. "Why don't you cut to the chase?"

"Because we're playing." He tickled her belly and ribs, down over her mound to her soft inner thigh. In spite of her-self, Kennedy flinched.

"Maybe a tiny bit ticklish?" Sam said.

"You get hard. I get wet," Kennedy said. "Is your toy waterproof?"

Sam moved in so close, she could feel his hot breath against her face. "You are *not* so tough."

"Wanna bet?" she taunted.

She heard him step back, imagined the sweep of his gaze honing in on her V Zone, and excitement shot through her. Little prickles of want blossomed into droplets of dew. "I can't touch you, Sam, but I want to. Come over here and slip your cock in my mouth." She outlined her lips with her tongue and heard the hiss of his indrawn breath. "I bet you're hard. I bet you're aching."

She jumped when a light drizzle of warm oil hit her skin.

Sam kissed her hard, as if to keep her quiet. "Hush, Kennedy, or I'll gag you."

She laughed against his lips. "You'd never do that! You'd miss hearing my screams as you pleasure me."

"Who says I intend to pleasure you?" His hands sleeked across her skin, rubbing in the oil.

"We'll see." She undulated beneath his touch as the heat from his oil-slicked palms singed a path across her skin.

She heard his sexy throaty chuckle. "I had my doubts any sort of restraints could keep you still for long."

She rolled her hips from side to side.

Abruptly the mask was lifted from her eyes. Sam stood naked before her in the juncture of her legs, his cock ramrod straight, jutting toward her.

"You look good enough to eat," she purred.

"What am I going to do with you?"

"You tell me. I'm your prisoner."

Justine

Sexcapades

collect:

- ☑ your date's boxers
- ☑ his favorite golf glove
- ☑ a snip of his chest hair

score:

- — a shooter he slurps from your belly button
- — an extravagant piece of jewelry
- — a picture of his penis

enjoy:

- — sex in a limo
- ☑ water sex (indoors or out)
- ☑ sex outdoors (double points for daytime)
- ☑ skinny-dipping with your date
- — dress-up sex
- — him as your slave, bondage included
- — *Spending the night together*

Chapter Ten

$\mathcal{J}$ustine, who'd never been to a spa before, didn't know where to look first as she followed Olivia up the curving staircase and along a dim corridor to double wooden doors. Inside, Olivia showed her where to hang her robe.

"Enjoy your massage," she said before she drifted soundlessly back the way they had come.

Alone, Justine wondered if it was normal to have two massage tables, side by side. Shrugging out of her robe, she lay facedown on the closest table, took a few deep breaths, and tried to relax.

"Madam, I am Charles." She jumped when she heard a male voice at her shoulder. Did the people who worked here all move like ghosts?

"If madam would be so kind as to accept this special eye pad."

Justine propped herself on her elbows and positioned the cool pad across her eyes as he tied it behind her head.

"Perfect. Have you had a couples treatment before?"

"A *what*? I think there's been some mistake."

"No mistake." She heard the rustle of movement and Eric's reassuring voice next to her. "Relax and enjoy the attentions of two men."

"I shall start with the gentleman," Charles announced. Justine heard Eric's deep sigh of contentment. "Justine, you're going to love this."

She shifted on her table, the skin of her back prickling in anticipation, hungry to be touched. She didn't have long to wait before capable, competent hands spread oil across her skin and skillfully honed in on the tightly knotted muscles of her shoulders and back.

"Doesn't that feel good?" Eric asked.

Any sort of answer required effort. "Divine." She sighed.

"Just wait," Eric promised.

Charles moved around the table to her feet and massaged her toes and ankles, up to her calves. As his hands slid up her legs she felt herself getting turned on. How was that possible with another man's hands on her body?

"Eric?"

"I'm here. Your skin is like satin in the candlelight."

Charles stood between their two beds and she could tell he had one hand on her and one on Eric.

If she was getting turned on, how was Eric doing?

She heard the shifting of movement. "What are you doing?" she asked Eric.

"I'm right here." And he was, standing at the end of the table attending her feet, while Charles at the opposite end was massaging her back and arms.

She did enjoy the attention of two men at once: the professional touch of the massage therapist in tandem with the caress of her lover.

She felt Eric's hands slide higher between her legs. Her clit throbbed and pulsed; her muscles grew slack, yet everything within her tightened. How could she be so tense and so relaxed at the same time? Was Charles watching? Internal and external conflicts went to war. She craved sexual release, yet was determined to behave appropriately.

When warm, questing hands slid beneath her sides and caressed her breasts, she made no move to stop them or worry who touched her. It felt so good. A stab of pleasure tweaked from her nipples to her V Zone, a fresh outpouring of sweet hot need between her legs.

"Stop!" She batted the hands away. "I can't. I—"

"It's okay, we're alone."

"Oh, thank goodness."

Eric's fingers nuzzled her nest. She was so wet, so needful. She rubbed against him. It was past time to be ashamed of her actions. She raised her hips, urging him closer. Was that his chest sliding the length of her back? His cock rooted and she raised her hips to accommodate him, then felt the hot relief of him slowly filling her. He nibbled her shoulder, licked the back of her neck, and massaged her breasts as she indulged in the slow, sensual burn to ecstasy.

"We have a special treat in store for you," Olivia told Lisa as she ushered her into the dimly lit room.

"What's that?" Lisa looked around her in amazement, and focused on the massage table, which was extra wide and four-poster.

Olivia pointed to a curtained changing area. "You're accustomed to following the lead of others, correct? This is your opportunity to take charge."

Inside the cubicle, Lisa gasped at the sight of the waiting costume: a shiny, brief black bustier, black stockings, and high black boots. It was so ludicrously unlike anything she ever envisioned for herself that she was intrigued. She held the garment against her and studied her reflection, her eyes bright with excitement.

Go ahead, whispered a tiny inner voice. *Try it on.*

Once she was cinched in, the bustier exaggerated her curves and her breasts spilled from a top cut so low that the shadowy crests of her nipples were partly visible. She stepped back and studied her reflection, barely recognizing the woman in the mirror, pale hair, her eyes wide and bright. In keeping with the pose, she put on red lipstick, then narrowed her eyes sternly. Gone was good-girl Lisa, who always did what she was told. In her place . . .

She stepped into the main room, her heart beating a staccato in her chest as she wondered who, or what, might be lying in wait for her.

Richard looked up at her and smiled in approval, his gaze gliding over her.

"Richard." She faltered at the sight of him, her stride hesitant.

"Well, well," he said. "Look at you."

"What are you doing here?"

His voice was husky and low, daring her. "Whatever you want me to do."

Excitement heightened the heady sense of power and thrummed through her veins. She threw her shoulders back, emphasizing the thrust of her breasts. Her stride grew more confident as she closed the distance between them. "Strip," she said in a voice she barely recognized as her own. "Then lie down on your back."

He shrugged from his robe and did as he was told.

A side table held an array of props and she picked through them till she found what she wanted. Silk scarves, soft yet strong. She lashed Richard's hands to the posts of the table, leaning over him so the tips of her breasts brushed his chest. A jolt of pleasure stole her breath, prickles of awareness nesting in the juncture of her legs, and she gave the knot an extra hard tug.

"Careful," Richard said. He was fully aroused and hers to do with as she wished.

"I'm always careful." And wasn't that the problem?

She found a device with a stiff handle attached to a dozen or so long suede fringes. It looked ominous, but wouldn't hurt. She swished it through the air in his direction. Did he actually flinch? Surely he knew she would never hurt him. Or did he? Did he want to be hurt?

"I wouldn't have taken you as submissive," she said, trailing the suede fringes across his torso toward his straining cock.

"I'm open to new things. But only pleasure, not pain."

"Agreed." She circled the table. "As long as you do what I say."

"How could I refuse you?"

"You can't." She joined him on the table and straddled his middle, inching up till her breasts were near his mouth. "Suck my breasts."

The tip of his tongue just barely made contact with her exposed nipples. "Harder." She purposefully kept her distance, making him do the work: raise his head, clamp her breast, and tug it deep into his mouth. Her nipple tightened into a hard knot of pleasure against his probing tongue. Her inner lips grew moist and she widened her legs, rubbing against him, enjoying the stimulation.

She straightened and shimmied forward, unable to believe her own boldness and the excitement she was getting from being in charge. "Taste me."

Her eyes on his, she opened herself so his tongue could lap at her tiny pleasure pearl, sending shock waves of delight through her. She leaned forward and grasped one corner post, using the leverage to move with him and against him.

It felt good.

It felt bad.

Finally she reared up in a cry of release and surrender as waves of a climax undulated through her, cresting into more intense orgasmic swells that finally left her weak and trembling. She barely managed to reach up and untie his hands.

"And now?" His breath rose and fell in time with hers, his cock pulsing with need.

She trailed her fingers along his length, heard him suck in his breath. "Stand over there and finish yourself while I watch."

He blanched. "Are you sure?"

Power and control surged through her. She flicked the suede toy, its tails cracking the air between them. "Very sure."

She watched as he clamped a hand around his erect cock. Slowly he stroked its length and she watched, fascinated by the way the skin shifted beneath his touch, flushing a deep pink. A fresh outpouring of moisture dampened her V Zone. She clamped her legs together, further inflaming her senses.

She'd always wondered, when she touched Les, if she had been doing it right. He'd always mumbled that it was fine, but he hadn't seemed to like her touching him; he was more anxious to plunge inside her and get it over with as quickly as possible.

Not like Richard. She could see a teardrop of moisture seep from the eye of his cock and he spread it like lubricant, his chest rising and falling, his breath coming in short, harsh spurts as he increased his hand speed.

"What are you thinking about?" she asked him.

"About you—touching yourself while you watch me."

"Really?" A surge of excitement darted through her.

"First your breasts."

"Like this?" She laid her palms flat atop her nipples where they spilled over the top of her cinched bustier, all rosy and responsive. Slowly she moved her hands in circles, enjoying her own touch.

Richard's breath caught. His hand faltered on his cock, then resumed. "Yeah." His voice wasn't quite steady. "Then your pussy. All wet and sweet."

She parted her legs.

He licked his lips, almost as if he could taste her. "I can see it glistening. Stroke it."

She reached down and touched herself, so hot, so sensitive, she had to use the lightest touch, ringing the inner lips, feeling them swell. Her clit twitched as she barely grazed it with her thumb. She dipped one finger inside, then two, in and out, her thumb working her clit harder and faster as Richard pumped his length.

He closed his eyes as semen spurted from his cock, and he exhaled with a ragged sigh of relief.

It was her turn to sigh. "I was just thinking it might be nice to have you inside me."

"Give me a couple of minutes, and that can be arranged."

While Kennedy's lack of control proved amazingly freeing, it was also extremely frustrating. She undulated as Sam stood between her legs staring down at her, quivering in anticipation. All he had to do was take a half step forward, to slide that gorgeous dick of his inside her. She was soaking wet with excitement, throbbing, savoring the anticipation of him filling her. The first thrust would be so incredible, it would probably take her up and over.

She wanted him, and she wanted him now!

"What are you waiting for?" she taunted. "You know you want me."

He smiled a self-assured smile and slowly shook his head. "Unlike you, my beautiful one, I have not only control, but self-control." He turned and walked away.

Kennedy sputtered in amazement. "You can't just walk away and leave me like this."

"You're right." He flicked a sheet across her nakedness. "See you around, Kennedy."

Kennedy yelled and swore after him, tugging at her restraints, but he was gone.

Eventually Olivia glided in and released her. "A new experience for you? That is our specialty here at Elements."

Kennedy sat up rubbing her wrists. "He'll pay for that, the bastard."

The night of the Gala Justine stared at herself in the full-length mirror in her room at the villa. "You're a fake."

She felt better having said it aloud. She faked it quite well in front of her friends, pretending she belonged here.

In truth, she had no clue who she was; not even her name was her own. Her father hadn't stuck around long enough to give her his, and when her mother had finally met some other loser, she'd stuck Justine with that name so they'd all match. Pretending to be a real family.

The baby she longed for would have a father, a name it could be proud of. The baby would be all hers, and give her an identity. A purpose.

"Justine. Are you ready?" Lisa knocked on her door.

"Just about." She clipped on the earrings that were part of tonight's costume, took a breath, and flung open her door. "Ta-dah!"

"Wow!" Her friends' approval was a balm to her feelings. She hoped to see that same approval in Eric's eyes, but after the spa, who knew what he thought of her?

The red dress enhanced her skin and eyes, and her hair had been fashioned in a simple, elegant twist. Growing up dirt-poor, she'd never dared dream of herself in a gown like this, rubbing shoulders with rich and influential people.

Kennedy's eyes searched her face. "What's up, girl?"

Damn, what had she given away? "Just wondering if Eric might be there."

"Most likely." Kennedy shrugged one smooth, creamy shoulder and tossed her head. "I know Sam's going with a date."

"How do you feel about that?" Lisa asked.

"I couldn't care less."

Justine didn't buy Kennedy's bravado, and it was an enlightening moment. Could her friend be as much of a fake as she was underneath? "Just don't either of you abandon me," she said. "This is my first time at a fancy affair like this."

"Come on," Kennedy said. "You've hobnobbed with tons of 'beautiful people' over the years."

"Wrong," Justine said. "I've designed their homes. I

worked for them. I was never one of them." And when she was out and about, she was never unescorted. Mr. Married had seen to that.

"Tonight, my friends, is our night to shine," Kennedy said.

Justine wished she could borrow some of Kennedy's confidence and style. "I can't believe you rented a limo to take us to the Gala." She stared at the elegant white stretch parked in front of their villa, wanting to freeze this moment in time.

A tuxedoed driver opened the rear door and she followed her friends into the opulent leather interior, where an ice bucket held a bottle of champagne, ringed by crystal flutes. "I feel like royalty!" Justine said.

"One of life's lessons." Kennedy leaned forward to fill their champagne glasses. "If you act like somebody, people will assume you're somebody. Appearances are everything."

"So we let people wonder who these three gorgeous women are, arriving by limo? Are we celebrities? Are we royalty?"

"Exactly."

Justine sipped her champagne and felt an overwhelming surge of love and gratitude for her friends. Not only did they accept her as she was, they took her with them on life's ride.

They arrived at the Royale Yacht Club a short time later, where the limo driver queued in the line of taxis and cars waiting to discharge their passengers. Justine leaned forward as they got close. "Oh, my word. There's even a red carpet to walk on."

"Smile, and act like you've been doing this all your life," Kennedy said.

Their vehicle inched forward until finally the driver stopped the car and got out to open their door.

Arms linked, the trio made their way up the red carpet and into the foyer of the Yacht Club, where potted plants, their branches twined with twinkling white lights, gave an air of festivity to the evening. A crush of people mingled inside the entrance foyer, drinks in hand, while a jazz trio played in the far corner.

Two attractive, young, white-jacketed waiters tripped over each other in their haste to bring drinks to them. Justine accepted hers with a gracious nod, then turned to survey the assembled crowd, an interesting mix of all ages.

"What's this event raising funds for?" Justine asked Kennedy.

"Senior care," Kennedy said. "It's not exactly a glamorous charity, but it is a fact of life. And with more and more people retiring to the area, they need good facilities."

"OMIGOD! Is that who I think it is?"

Kennedy followed Justine's line of vision to a famous actor. "I heard he was a big supporter." She tugged on Lisa's arm. "I see lots of pro golfers. Your friend Richard was probably instrumental in getting them here tonight."

Lisa colored and glanced around. "I wonder where he is."

Justine broke away from her friends and made her way toward a familiar figure. Even with his back to her, she'd recognize Eric anywhere.

She tapped him on the shoulder and he turned.

"Justine." He looked surprised to see her. "I didn't know you'd be here tonight. I heard it sold out months ago."

She smiled. "A girl just needs to know the right people."

"And the right people are all here tonight."

At that moment, the woman standing next to Eric turned their way and Justine's mouth dropped, her eyes riveted to the woman's belly. She had to be a good seven months pregnant—and there was no mistaking the fond way she looked at Eric. "Aren't you going to introduce us?"

"Certainly," Eric said calmly. "Justine this is my . . . this is—"

"I'm Anne," the woman finished for him, extending a hand toward Justine. "Eric and I used to be married."

"Justine," she managed to get out, as the still-functioning area of her brain registered the fact that Anne had a nice, firm handshake.

"Have you two known each other long?" Anne asked conversationally.

Somehow Justine managed to shake her head, punctuating Eric's terse "No."

Anne ran a loving hand across her abdomen. "I know I'm huge for seven months, but it's twins," she said happily.

"C-congratulations," Justine stammered, glancing about for some means of escape. "I'd better get back to my friends. I don't remember which table we're at."

"It was terrific of you to come out and support the Senior Care Society," Anne said.

Justine managed to nod before she left.

She bolted right past Lisa and Kennedy. Lisa grabbed her arm and pulled her in. "What's the matter? You look like you've seen a ghost."

"Eric. His ex. She's pregnant," Justine blurted out. "With twins."

"How unfortunate," Kennedy said. "Come on, they've opened the ballroom doors. Let's go find our table."

Justine took a long, steadying breath. *Get a grip,* she told herself. *The evening is not ruined. In fact, it's familiar territory.*

Inside the ballroom, the men were all in tuxes or white dinner jackets, the women all turned out to the nines. With a built-in homing instinct, Kennedy steered them to their table. "Put your evening bag down so that we have seats, then off we go to mingle."

Justine cast an envious glance at her friends, so easy in their element. Lisa had been born to this life and Kennedy had adopted it with ease, while she . . . She deserved this, she told herself. And she wasn't about to let Eric's presence rob her of any pleasure.

"Oh, look," Kennedy squealed. "The Diamond King."

As Kennedy scampered off, Justine leaned toward Lisa. "Who or what is a Diamond King?"

"I don't know. But I just spotted Richard at that table near the front. Eric's with him."

"At least Richard isn't with someone carrying twins," Justine said.

"I can't tell who he's with. You look. I don't want him to see me staring."

"I can't look," Justine said. "Eric will think I'm looking at him. Where's Kennedy? She can spy for both of us."

"I'm right here, girls."

"Whoa!" Justine recoiled from the blaze of diamonds that

encircled Kennedy's neck, ending in one huge stone nestled between her breasts.

"Suits me, don't you think?" Kennedy preened, admiring the way the gems caught the light. "Come on, he's got more."

"What do you mean he's got more?"

"It's Diamond Jim Braidy, the Diamond King. He brings his gems and gives people in the crowd the opportunity to wear them for part of the evening."

"Doesn't he worry about theft?"

"Never. The place is crawling with security."

Justine trailed after her friends, trying to look as if several million dollars' worth of diamonds was nothing new.

"Lisa, the tiara," Kennedy insisted, pushing her friend toward the large man sporting a white tuxedo.

"Your friend has good taste," he said, flashing a grin that revealed a gold front tooth imbedded with a diamond. "Fit for a princess." His assistant secured the tiara onto Lisa's head, and he pulled Lisa and Kennedy alongside him to pose for a photo. Justine's attention was drawn to an exquisite bracelet, heavy with diamonds.

The assistant fastened it around her wrist. "It was made for you. It shows off your beautiful hands."

"Thank you." She'd always thought she had particularly nice hands, with slim, shapely wrists and elegantly tapered fingers, but this was the first time anyone had ever said as much.

Lisa cast a surreptitious glance toward the front of the room, wondering if Richard had noticed her yet. Kennedy had launched into a mini press conference with the local TV journalist and photographer so subtly the journalist had no idea what was going on.

Why couldn't she be more like that? Ballsy enough to go after her dream? But even if she was brave enough to go after something, what did she really want? Not to fall hard for the first man she met. She needed to have fun, sow a few wild oats.

Justine tapped her arm, pulling her out of her reverie. "I'm going to the ladies' room. I'll be right back."

Lisa nodded, and raised one hand to her head. She had the tiara. So where was her prince?

Justine admired the stunning flash of light on the diamond bracelet as she washed and dried her hands. She'd always thought of herself as a pearl girl, but there was something powerful and hypnotic about the cold, heavy sparkle of dia-monds. Maybe there just needed to be enough of them.

She was about to leave the ladies' room when she heard a muffled sob coming from one of the cubicles. She paused. Whoever it was obviously wanted to be alone, but something in her couldn't just leave.

She cleared her throat. The crying got louder.

"Uh, I don't mean to intrude, but are you okay in there? Would you like me to get someone?"

There was a muffled, "I'll be okay," followed by the sound of vigorous nose blowing.

"Do you want me to wait?"

The toilet flushed. The door opened, and out waddled

pregnant Anne. She gave Justine a watery smile. "Hormones," she said by way of explanation. "I hear it's worse with twins."

"I heard that too," Justine said.

"Do you have children?" Anne asked as she blotted her eyes then splashed cold water on her face.

Justine quickly shook her head. "Not yet."

"Careful what you wish for." Anne rested one hand on her stomach. "I wanted this to the exclusion of everything else in my life. Including my husband."

"Is your husband here tonight?"

"No. He's overseas with the military. I don't know if he'll be back in time or not. I'm lucky to have Eric as my birth coach."

"He is?" Justine tried to keep her voice even.

"Ironic, isn't it? We get along so much better now that we're not married."

"And your current husband doesn't mind?"

"He knows that I still love Eric and always will; we just don't talk about it."

"Does Eric know you still love him?"

"Of course—we don't have any secrets from each other. Just lots of regrets. Eric tells me you and your friends are visiting from the Pacific Northwest."

Justine nodded. "We're just here for a short vacation."

"You were lucky to get tickets to tonight's event."

"That's what everyone tells us."

What else had Eric told Anne about her, Justine wondered as they made their way back to the ballroom.

Once there, she watched Anne take her place alongside Eric at one of the VIP tables.

How many times in the past had she been at a social event, a fake date on her arm, eyes glued to her lover and his wife in the elite inner circle, pining to be that woman, not the dirty little secret in the back of the room?

Woodenly, she plopped herself next to Lisa. "What did I miss?"

"Everything!" Lisa was bubbling with far more animation than Justine had seen in a long time. "Look at that table over there against the wall. Do you see him?"

"See who?" Justine asked.

"Ted October! He's here, in the flesh!"

"What are you talking about? There is no Ted October."

"Oh yes there is, and Kennedy's talking to him. Look— he's getting up and coming over!"

Justine's heart missed a beat. Lisa was right. It was the same face as on that long-ago calendar, even more gorgeous in real life. Wavy chocolate hair, chiseled jaw, white smile, and bedroom eyes.

"Girls." Kennedy presented him with a flourish. "Meet Ted." She pointed. "Ted, this is Justine and this is Lisa. We're all big fans of your work."

At that moment the lights dimmed, and the MC stepped up to the podium. With an apologetic shrug and a promise to see them all later, Ted returned to his seat.

The MC introduced their guest of honor, a retired celebrity golfer who was heartily welcomed. As the applause died down, he launched into a touching speech about the Senior Care Society and what they were doing to ensure dignity and comfort for the community's elderly citizens.

He was a good speaker, witty and eloquent, but Lisa couldn't concentrate. She'd spotted Richard at one of the VIP tables with Eric. He looked happy and relaxed, and she didn't notice any woman, so perhaps he was here alone. He hadn't seen her yet.

Her gaze strayed from him to Ted October, and a wicked idea blossomed Since he'd met bad-girl Lisa at the spa the other day, perhaps she ought to seize this chance to make Richard jealous.

Chapter Eleven

*O*nce the meal was cleared away, Lisa propped her chin in her hands as she scanned the crowded room. "I remember hating these black-tie fund-raising dinners," she said. "Stuck in your seat for hours next to a bunch of stuffed shirts, every-one wanting something."

"Ever think maybe it was the company you were with?" Kennedy drawled.

"I love this. It's fantastic people watching," Justine said. "But then, I'm new to it."

"Usually I wound up sitting at a table full of phonies."

"That's because you were there with your husband. And not to speak ill of the dead, but wasn't he the biggest phony of all?"

"He was a user." It had stung when Les told her he married her because she had the right pedigree and was the wife he needed to complete the portrait of success he portrayed to the business world, but not worthy of his love or his loyalty.

"The way I see it, these people can be of use to us," Kennedy said.

"How so?" asked Justine.

Before Kennedy had a chance to answer, the MC was back at the mike and the live auction began. Richard still hadn't noticed Lisa and she was piqued about that. He hadn't mentioned his role tonight. But even if he knew she was here, would she be just another accessory to complete the picture? She'd had enough of that. More than enough.

Eventually the auction ended, the dance band took up their instruments, and couples drifted onto the dance floor at the front of the room. Lisa tapped her foot restlessly.

"Don't you think it's weird that Ted's here?" Justine asked.

Lisa shrugged. "It's a crazy small world. But I think it's time I asked him to dance." She pushed to her feet and crossed the room, purpose in every stride.

Ted saw her coming and rose to meet her, flashing that million megawatt smile. Lisa felt the room and people fade into the background as Ted took her hand. Words were unnecessary compared to being in his arms. This is what she'd been missing, Lisa realized. A man who made her feel like a princess. Ted was so tall she couldn't see over his shoulder to know whether or not Richard had spotted her. But how could he not? It felt like all eyes were on the two of them, him so dark and dashing, her so fair and glittery, their bodies in sync as if they'd been dancing together forever.

Justine caught a speculative look on Kennedy's face and reached across to get her friend's attention. "Lisa looks terrific. Happier than I've seen her in forever. This trip was the best thing ever."

"I can't help but wonder how our little Cinderella feels about the society pages." Kennedy indicated a woman with a camera aimed at Lisa and Ted.

"Excuse me, ladies. Did you call your friend Cinderella? Because that's exactly the hook I'm looking for."

Kennedy turned. "And you are?"

"Tracy Holmes. *The Daily Dispatch*."

Kennedy instantly morphed into Ms. Public Relations. "Pleasure to meet you. Have I got a story for you!"

Justine leaned forward. "Are you sure you want to do this, Kennedy?"

"It's all in keeping with the tone of our trip."

Kennedy regaled the reporter with her story of three girl-friends on a mission to rekindle belief in happy endings, capped by the unexpected appearance of their "ideal man." At the reporter's insistence, the three girls posed with Ted, together and individually, before Ted took a turn on the dance floor with each one.

*   *   *

Lisa watched Kennedy laughing up at Ted across the room. Nearby, Justine was dancing with Eric. She'd gone from being the center of attention to invisibility. Had her princess gown turned to rags without her noticing?

"You look a little lost."

"Richard." Her heart gave a happy leap that he'd sought her out.

"I just came over to tell you how beautiful you look. Like a fairy-tale princess."

So why was she feeling locked in an ivory tower?

"It's quite a change from the last time I saw you," he said. She blushed in memory of her dominatrix role-playing at the spa, but Richard's eyes twinkled. "I guess we all need to learn we can't always have control over things."

"You seem very busy tonight," she replied coolly. Did he get the underlying message? That he'd neglected her and forgiveness was not forthcoming?

"I try to arm-twist some of the big names into supporting the cause. Who's the calendar boy?"

"Isn't that obvious? He's the man of our dreams."

She had a vague suspicion he was trying hard not to laugh.

"So if I were to ask you out afterward, I don't have a hope?"

"That's right," she said. "Ted has a prior claim."

As if on cue, Ted appeared and cinched an arm around her waist. "Darling, they're playing our song."

"So they are." She gave Richard her sweetest smile. "Nice to see you."

"Likewise," Richard said.

Each time Ted twirled or dipped her in Richard's direction, she couldn't help looking to see if he was watching. Unfortunately, he wasn't.

The party was kicking into high gear, and Kennedy was mentally congratulating herself on the success of her scheme when she ran into Sam.

She attempted to brush past him with a cool smile, but he moved to block her path.

"You three are certainly the belles of the ball tonight."

"We're having fun. How about you?"

He gave her a funny little smile, as if he saw more than she wanted him to. "Do you have a minute? There's someone here I'd like you to meet."

His date! The nerve!

Her first instinct was to refuse. Didn't he know she still hadn't forgiven him for that time at the spa? Stripping her control? It wouldn't happen again.

"Please," he added, as if sensing her refusal.

"I guess for a minute," she said with poor grace.

The special way he smiled down at her did weird melty things she didn't like to her insides. She was wrestling with that confusion when he compounded it by linking her fingers through his in an intimate way as he guided her across the room to a table where a smartly dressed older woman sat watching their progress.

"Kennedy, I'd like you to meet my mother, Lillian. Mother, this is Kennedy."

Lillian took her other hand. "It's a pleasure, my dear. I was nagging Sam to find someone to dance with, and he finally confessed that the only woman in the room he wanted to dance with was you. I insisted he bring you over to meet me the second you were free."

"Mother, are you all right here by yourself if I give Kennedy a twirl? You're not too tired?"

"Pshaw. I'll be fine. You young people run along and have fun."

Kennedy felt the possessive warmth of Sam's hand on the small of her back as he led her to the dance floor. "So when you told me earlier that you had a special date, it was your mother. Why didn't you just tell me that?"

"It didn't seem important."

Kennedy eyed him speculatively. Sam didn't seem the type to play games. So why did she get the sense that he'd enjoyed unsettling her?

"I bring her to this event every year. She enjoys getting out, and the cause is dear to her heart."

"She's lovely." It was impossible to avoid the comparison to "Mommy Dearest" who wouldn't be caught dead at a charity fund-raiser unless there was something pretty darn big in it for her.

"She's a lot more frail than she lets on, and despite what she says, she's tiring. So we'll be leaving soon." He trailed his hand along her bare shoulder and back. "I'd like to see you later. What are you doing afterward?"

"The girls and I made plans to go out on the town."

"I understand." Was there a coolness as he released her at

the end of the song? "I won't keep you, then. Thank you for coming to meet my mother."

Kennedy nodded and moved to step away, when he caught her hand and held her in place. "What's wrong?" he asked quietly.

She avoided that gaze that seemed to see right inside her. "Nothing. Why?"

He shook his head. "I know you, Kennedy. Better than you think." With a final squeeze of her fingers, he let her go. She watched him make his way to his mother, bend down to speak to her, then lift her in his arms and carry her to a discreetly positioned wheelchair.

She stood frozen in shock as Sam lovingly tucked a robe over his mother's knees and wheeled her from the party. On his heels she saw Eric escorting his pregnant ex-wife. How had this happened? She and her friends were supposed to meet players, good-time partyers—not real caring men with families and feelings.

"You coming, Kennedy?"

The sight of Justine and Lisa, one on either side of Ted, was enough to shake her out of her funk. "You bet!"

Kennedy was right, Justine mused, being the center of attention was fun, even in borrowed finery and jewels. She didn't even mind when it was time to return the bracelet and climb back into their pumpkin—in this case, the limo with Ted.

Kennedy leaned forward to talk to their driver. "Take us to the wildest club in town."

The driver turned around, gave them a long hard look. "Can you handle wild?"

"We need something a lot more happening than where we just were."

They drove around for a while, talking and laughing about nothing in particular till the limo drew to a stop in front of a dark building on the edge of town. There was no sign, no one lined up, nothing to indicate a late-night club. Stairs descended from street level into a dark cubby.

"This is it?" Kennedy said in disbelief.

"It's the most exclusive club on the island. You need a password to get in." He wrote something down and passed it to her.

"Just what kind of club is it?"

"You'll see."

Kennedy led the way down the stairs to a large medieval-looking wooden door with a grate in it and rang the bell. A small panel slid open behind the grate, and a pair of eyes stared out at her. She repeated the password. After what felt like forever, she heard the lock release and the door swung open.

A pale, thin young man dressed all in black with more piercings than Kennedy could count gave them the once-over in an unsettling way. Kennedy couldn't hear a sound except her friends shuffling out of their coats. Where was the music, the noise, the excitement she craved?

"You'll need these." He handed each of them a garish mask on a stick. Kennedy held hers up and her vision was instantly distorted.

"What do we need these for?"

"The regulars have their own. These are for out-of-town guests."

"Everyone at this club wears a mask?"

He gave her a look that said he was disgusted by her ignorance. Then he opened an inner door which was obviously soundproof, for instantly Kennedy was assaulted by noise and music. She stepped boldly over the threshold into a huge, dark cave-like room.

She positioned the mask across her eyes, and was able to make out lights and shapes. It was like looking through a tunnel: she could see ahead, but not peripherally. She had the feeling that without the mask she wouldn't be able to see at all. Together they converged on an empty table and chairs. Once seated, she turned to the others. "I take it back; this is more than wild."

"I've heard of these clubs, but never been to one," Ted said.

The doorman had been right. Everyone wore a mask: some simple, some bizarrely elaborate with feathers and beaks or oversize glittery spectacles.

Kennedy turned her attention to the tableau on stage, where a full-gear dominatrix disciplined several people. Dark doorways were set into alcoves around the room, and although she couldn't see what went on in the shadows, she had a good enough imagination.

When a punk-looking waitress in skimpy attire arrived to take their drink order, Ted ordered champagne all around.

"Smart," Kennedy said. "You wouldn't want to order a mixed-drink here; you never know what someone might put into it."

"What do you mean?" Lisa asked.

"Sweetheart, you are so naive. Look. Listen. Learn."

"But this can't be real," Lisa said. "These people are actors, right? This is staged."

"I wouldn't bet on it."

"I don't think this is my scene," Justine said, shifting uncomfortably.

Music pulsed in time to the flashing strobe light, giving macabre illumination to the crush of bodies dancing in the center of the room. Extreme fetishes danced with traditional-garbed men and women, a touching, sensory skin-fest.

"Come on." Kennedy urged Ted and her friends to their feet. "When in Rome . . ."

Justine and Lisa stuck together like wooden puppets, but a wild streak raced through Kennedy as she absorbed the energy of the club. All those years of dance lessons when she was young hadn't been wasted; she could dance and she loved it. Shimmying up to Ted, she ran her hands all over his body in slow intimacy, their gazes locked. After several intensely connected moments she slowly swung about and presented her back to him, hips swaying from side to side, getting closer and closer, till she felt his hands on her hips pulling her back against him, molding her shape. His palms slid over her ribs to her breasts and she ground back against him, felt his erection, stroked him through his trousers.

"Careful." He spoke directly in her ear before his lips sampled her lobe, then the skin of her neck.

It wasn't Ted!

"I hope you don't mind me cutting in."

"Come on," Justine said to Lisa. "Let's go look around."

"I don't know. . . ."

"Hey, we'll probably never be in an underground club like this again, given our sheltered lives."

"Sheltered? Not after this week."

"Kennedy wanted to shake us out of our comfort zone, and she sure went about it the right way."

"Don't let go of me."

"Trust me, I won't."

Masks in position, the girls held hands tightly as they wound through the underground labyrinth of alcoves and rooms.

Wall sconces flickered and lent a surreal shadowing in the alcove Justine stepped into, Lisa's hand clutching tightly to hers.

The masks gave everything an unreal purplish haze, but without the mask all you could see was shadowy movement. One woman and two men were involved in a ménage à trois, uncaring who watched. One of the men sat propped against the headboard of a huge bed, mounded with pillows. A woman sat cradled in his lap, her back to his chest. His arms were around her, large hands caressing her naked breasts as he kissed her neck, her face so blissful with pleasure that Justine felt her breathing accelerate as she watched.

The second man had his dark head buried between the

woman's pale legs, pleasuring her with his mouth while he caressed his enormous erection. The woman's moan of carnal pleasure rippled through Justine's limbs.

Lisa seemed rooted to the spot. "They don't care that others are watching," she whispered.

"Some people are exhibitionists, some are voyeurs." Justine shifted her gaze through the room, not surprised to see some of those watching beginning their own foreplay. She tugged at Lisa's hand. "Had enough?"

Lisa nodded, but seemed reluctant to rip her gaze from the scene.

The next group was a mass of gyrating bodies in orgy mode, which didn't interest Justine.

One small, dark cavern held a hot tub where two beautiful young women cavorted in the gently pulsating water.

One climbed up to perch on the edge of the tub, her legs splayed as she pleasured herself. Meanwhile, her friend appeared to ride one of the jets of water while a small gaggle of onlookers of both genders watched, fascinated.

Justine and Lisa looked at each other, shrugged, and moved on.

"Do you think couples come here, get turned on, then go home and get down?" Lisa asked.

"Maybe. If they even wait to get home."

"It reminds me of our spa day."

Justine flushed. "That was as wild as I ever need to be."

"I liked it," Lisa said. "It was me, but it wasn't me. And I don't know that I'll ever be that 'me' again, but at the time it seemed absolutely right."

They returned to their table to find Ted sitting alone.

"There you are. I wondered if you'd gotten caught up someplace," he said.

"Just looking around. Where's Kennedy?"

Ted pointed to the dance floor, where Kennedy gyrated in a most provocative manner against a man wearing a Zorro mask.

"He cut in on me," Ted said. "I think maybe she still thinks it's me."

Chapter Twelve

"Sam! What are you doing here?"

"I have a friend who's an undercover cop. He saw you all come in and he called me. He was worried about you."

"You don't think I can take care of myself?"

"Of course you can, but why should you have to?"

"That's what I do." And always had. Kennedy ground her teeth in frustration. He'd been in her way since the very first—unpredictable, catching her off guard and unawares. She still hadn't forgiven him for that day in the spa. Didn't he realize that if she had no control, she had nothing? "You're ruining all my plans."

He laughed behind the mask. "You mean things aren't turning out the way you want? News flash! You can't orchestrate other people's lives."

"Do you want to bet? Ted is here because of me. He was my trump card to take Lisa's and Justine's minds off those losers they used to be hooked up with."

He stopped dancing and speared her with his gaze. "So what's on your mind that you're trying so desperately to forget?"

"Nothing!" It was a lie of course. There were all those new twenty-something wonder kids at work. All young and fresh and enthusiastic, nipping at her aging heels. She turned the attention back to him. "Since you have your own mask, I assume you're a regular here. You needn't have rushed to my rescue, but do have fun while you're here."

She returned to the table just in time to see the others get up. "Where do you think you're going?" she asked.

"Sorry, Kennedy." Justine spoke up. "This isn't really our scene. You stay and have fun, though. We'll catch up with you at the villa."

She opened her mouth in protest, then closed it. Why did she need them here, anyway?

"Run along then." She dismissed them with a wave of her hand. "Never mind what I've done for you all. Just . . ." She peeked up through the eyeholes in her mask. They all seemed so far away, which she knew was an illusion. Or maybe it was more real than the truth. Maybe they *were* far away. Far enough that her guilt tactics wouldn't work. Was Sam right? Was she manipulative?

Things are not what they appear, she reminded herself as she poured a glass of champagne. She was simply used to getting things done. A certain way.

Sam slid into the empty chair across from her, and cocked his head in the direction of her departing friends. "None of my business, but you seem to do a bang-up job of driving people away. Especially if it looks like they might get too close."

She didn't want to have this conversation. She wanted to forget about everything, the way Sam had intimated. "Since you insist on being here, I insist you dance with me."

His grin widened behind his mask. "I thought you'd never ask."

She led the way to the dance floor, where she placed one hand on his shoulder and leaned in. "What happens next?"

"I'm here to help you win the sexcapades."

"I bet there's some hot wax around here someplace. We could get your chest waxed."

Her grip tightened on the stem of her mask. Distance was distorted. He was right there—yet he wasn't; it was almost as if she was seeing him underwater, or through a sheen of heat waves. Nothing seemed as it was. Not even Sam, as they danced, their bodies but a breath apart.

Sam shook his head, half admiringly, half in consternation. "You are a piece of work."

"I'm serious."

"I know you are. That's the scary part."

She nuzzled even closer, enjoying her sense of power. This was more the way it was supposed to be. "Are you scared, Sam?"

"Trembling in my boots."

She reached down and stroked his crotch, pleased to feel him harden against her hand. "Not exactly trembling."

"But most definitely intrigued."

She gave a loud purr in his ear; more tigress than kitten. "See, I thought I made this clear last time. I don't appreciate you showing up and taking charge."

"Oh, you like it just fine. You'll like it more when I fuck you in the limo. That's points for your sexcapades, is it not?"

She pulled back a little. "How do you know that?"

"I overheard the others. They elected not to leave the limo here for you."

"So what did you do?"

"I ordered a second limo."

She flashed him her most provocative smile. "Then what are we waiting for?"

Watching Lisa cozy up to Ted in the limo, Justine felt more alone than ever. She knew Lisa needed to sow her wild oats and Ted was the ideal candidate, but she was always the odd woman out.

She leaned forward and tapped the glass to get the driver's attention. "Can you take me to West Bay Marina?"

Lisa pulled her attention away from Ted. "What are you doing?"

"That's where Eric keeps his boat."

"Does he live on the boat?"

"No."

"Can you access the security gate?"

Justine shrugged. "I watched him punch in the code the other day."

"I bet you need a key card."

"You never know till you try." Justine nervously clenched her hands in her lap. She'd felt so special tonight dancing with Ted, and she wasn't willing to surrender those feelings—though it wasn't like her to be this bold, going after what she wanted. She could do it in business, no problem. Personal was different.

The limo glided through the marina parking lot and stopped at the gated entrance to the jetty. "We'll wait," Lisa said, and Justine felt a fresh surge of gratitude for the friendship.

"Thanks, but I'll be fine."

She approached the gated entrance with optimism, and gave a happy little skip when she found it unlatched, as if it was meant to be.

She spun around, flashed Lisa the thumbs-up, and let herself in, making her way to Eric's boat. She remembered where he kept the key and had few qualms as she unlocked the cabin and let herself in. The cabin was as cozy as she recalled. She kicked off her shoes, took off her borrowed dress, and slid under the duvet. The pillow smelled like Eric, and she inhaled deeply before she fell asleep.

Alone in the limo with Ted, Lisa decided to seduce him. Kennedy would be bold, provocative; she wouldn't wait for the guy to make the first move. When nuzzling up to him didn't seem to get any results, she kicked off her shoes, flung a leg across his lap, and wriggled around till she straddled him.

"Hey, you!" He flashed her that megawatt smile but caught her eager hands and prevented her from unbuttoning his shirt. She laughed, tugged free, and attacked a jacket button before he stopped her again.

Lisa pushed out her bottom lip in an exaggerated pout, adding what she hoped was a sexy little bounce in his lap. "I just want to touch you. All of you."

He cocked an eye toward their driver. "It's not very private here."

"Private enough to be naughty." She loosened his tie, and tucked her fingers inside the collar of his shirt. "Is that all right if I touch you?"

"Above the waist?"

She laughed. "You are so funny. And so sexy."

He ran his hands up the sides of her legs and under her bottom. She squealed aloud when he lifted her up and set her down next to him.

She ran her fingers up his arm. "Don't you like me, Ted?"

"I adore you, Lisa. But we're here."

She glanced out the window to the familiar lines of the villa. "So we are."

She grabbed her shoes and made her way barefoot up the front walk, making sure Ted had a full back view, giving her hips an extra swing.

She unlocked the door. "Miles. Oh, Miles," she sang out. "Come out, come out, wherever you are." She wove across the living room and dropped onto the couch, suddenly tired. She'd just close her eyes for a tiny minute.

She didn't know how long she'd been asleep, but she awoke disoriented, still on the couch. Someone had covered her with a couch throw. She sat up and blinked herself awake, disappointed but not surprised to find she was still fully clothed. Ted was obviously too much of a gentleman to take advantage of her inebriated state. She heard the faint sound of voices from the direction of the swimming pool.

The pool deck was dark, the underwater lights the only illumination. As she focused, she saw one shadowy figure turn into two, before the two entangled themselves back into one.

Ted and Miles. She backed away, making sure they didn't see her. She had a real gift for choosing the wrong man.

Justine batted away whatever was tickling her bare arm, but the sensation continued, gently pulling her from the divine dream she'd been having. She felt a puff of breath against her brow and reluctantly opened her eyes.

"Eric! What are you doing here?"

He laughed. "That was my question to you."

"Oh." As the gray fog lifted, she remembered where she was. "I hope you don't mind?"

"Finding a beautiful woman warming my bed? What's to mind?"

"Well, it was somewhat presumptuous of me to . . ."

His lips silenced hers, and it was a long time before he released her. "I like your presumption."

"Oh, good." She tangled her fingers through his hair and pulled him back for another long, lingering kiss.

He released her and pushed her tangled hair back from her face. "Did you and your friends have fun last night?"

"We always have fun."

"That was obvious. Who was the calendar boy you were all cozied up to?"

Justine nuzzled her cheek against his. "Long story, not all that interesting. Are you taking your clothes off and getting in here or what?"

"Let me think about that." He slowly pulled the duvet down inch by inch, exposing her to his view. Justine stretched, glad she was wearing a sexy bustier and the tiniest sheer scrap of panties.

Eric growled his approval, skimmed his hands across her midriff, and dragged the duvet down her thighs, stopping at her knees. Teasingly, he nudged her knees apart, smoothing his hands back up the insides of her thighs.

She gave a heartfelt sigh of approval at the warm weight of his hands on her.

"You're all toasty warm and relaxed from your sleep."

"I am." She moved against him, encouraging his continued exploration. He responded with the light brush of his fingertips across her mons, pressing one finger into the cleft.

"Your panties will get all wet. We should take them off."

She undulated against his hand. "We should." She lifted her hips while he made short work of discarding her panties.

"Bustier?" she asked.

"Leave it on. It's damn sexy." He traced the spillover of her breasts at the top of the garment, then raked his nails across the rigid nipples straining against the sheer fabric.

Justine sighed her pleasure. "Glad you like it."

Eric sprawled atop her and slowly slid down the length of her body, scattering kisses as he went. When he reached her feet, he pressed a hot kiss to each instep, tracing the arch with his tongue in a way that made her entire body shiver with pleasure, then slid her feet flat against the sheets so her knees were raised and open, exposing her inner pink palace.

As he teased and tongued the sensitive flesh Justine felt herself swell and simmer, first from the heat of his breath, then from the torturous pathway of his lips. She clenched the sheets as she rolled from side to side, her actions fueled by his. He took hold of her hips and held her still, transferring his attention to her soft inner thigh, leaving the inner sanctum throbbing with the need for release. A need he restoked with each swipe of his tongue, moving from inner thigh to inner lips in a leisurely fashion, teasing her to new heights. Her chest rose and fell with each straining breath as the pleasure built to a near unbearable pitch. When the crescendo hit she sobbed aloud with relief, feeling herself spill into him.

He knelt above her, approval in his eyes as he unfastened

the buckle of his belt and unzipped his jeans. She reached up to help, just as his cell phone rang.

"Leave it," she said.

"I can't. It might be Anne."

Justine felt herself deflate. Her arms fell to her sides as he checked the caller's number.

"It is Anne."

Chapter Thirteen

Giggling, Kennedy fell into the limo Sam had ordered, peering out the door to where Sam stood talking to their driver.

"I could have sex in here by myself, you know, but it defeats the intent of the sexcapades."

Sam slid in next to her and the door clicked shut. "What if I were to watch?"

"I didn't know you were into voyeurism. I thought you were into control."

"I'm open to anything. Anyway, I thought the intent of the sexcapades was to involve a variety of partners."

Kennedy gave an unladylike snort and realized she was more than a little tipsy. "Trust a man to think like that." She rolled toward him, flung her leg across one solid thigh. "The intent was for my friends to cut loose a little. That's all."

"But not you?"

Kennedy threw back her head and laughed. "I don't need anyone's encouragement to act outrageously."

"Even though I know you're not as outrageous as you try to pretend you are."

"Who's pretending?"

He leaned in close. "You might have your friends fooled, Kennedy, but not me."

She flopped back against her seat, arms folded across her chest. "You don't know me. No one does. Mommy Dearest's little Barbie doll: Wind her up and toss her away when you're done with her."

Kennedy caught herself abruptly, aware she was saying too much. She splayed across the leather seat and tugged the skirt of her dress up around her waist so she could part her legs for the show she planned to treat Sam to. She pushed down the bodice of her dress, freeing her breasts.

Sam obliged by shifting around so he had a better view.

"I love my breasts," Kennedy said, running her hands across their soft fullness. "Don't you?"

"They are spectacular," Sam agreed, his eyes darkening.

"No fakes," Kennedy said. "Not boobs or orgasms. I'm the real thing—in spite of Mommy Dearest."

"Where was your father?"

Kennedy gave a careless shrug and began stroking the insides of her thighs. "He didn't know about me yet. That was later. When I was eight. I guess I wasn't cute anymore. She got tired of dressing me up and playing with me."

She slid her fingers beneath the tiny panties she wore. "Does Sam want to play with me?"

Sam knelt between her legs, rubbing his face back and forth between her breasts, the slight abrasion of tomorrow's whiskers a stimulation that made her shiver.

"We've all got our stories, Kennedy."

"What's yours?" She tossed the words at him as a challenge.

"Something I'll share with you at some point. But right now I've got other things on my mind."

"So do I. Lie back." Kennedy gave him a push and he obligingly sprawled onto the floor of the vehicle. She slipped out of her panties and rose to stand over him, one leg on either side, even though she had to stoop slightly to manage it.

He looked up and smiled.

She smiled as well, dipped her fingers into the V Zone, and started to pet herself. She was wet and warm, heat turning hot as Sam's excitement grew, his breathing ragged.

Her hips swayed from side to side as she increased the speed at which her slick, wet fingers found their way through her inner folds to the center of her being.

Sam was a truly appreciative audience, his eyes meeting and matching hers, an approving half smile on his lips. She smiled back, confident in her power to arouse. Her breathing became faster and more labored, her eyes half closed with pleasure as she felt the preliminary tremors signaling the eruption that was soon to follow.

Faster and faster she dragged her middle finger across her clit, probed her inner sweetness, then back to her clit, circling it teasingly, adding a second, then a third finger to the mix, feeling herself swell and pulse, until with a harsh cry she climaxed. She collapsed onto Sam, fumbled with his belt, and ripped open his pants in frantic haste.

He sprang free, magnificently huge and hard, and she swiftly guided him inside her.

"Yes!" Sweet possession! Hands on his chest for support, she leaned forward, awash in relief at the way he surged into her, filling and stretching her, completing her in a way she had never been completed before.

"Don't stop now!"

Sam lay still beneath her.

She moved up and down; heard the hiss of his indrawn breath as he struggled for control. Abruptly, she stopped. "Is something wrong?"

It took him giving her all the control for her to realize that wasn't what she wanted. Did she only crave control when it looked like she might be losing it? A legacy from her early years when she had no control? Once it was freely given, handed over like right now, it no longer seemed important.

"I have something for you," she said softly. "Something I've never willingly given up before."

His eyes locked on hers, his expression suddenly serious. He knew without words what she meant.

He reached up and fondled her breasts. She gave a low murmur of approval deep in her throat. He pulled her forward and guided her breasts across his face, lashing at them with his tongue, till finally he caught them one at a time and gave a deep satisfying tug, a sensation that charged through her bloodstream and sent a fresh outpouring of damp heat to her inner chasm.

Sam exhaled heavily, positioned his hands on her hips to set the pace. "You are so hot."

Kennedy stretched her arms above her head, then arched her back, catching her weight behind her on Sam's legs, to explore a whole new angle of entry.

Her pleasure was Sam's sole responsibility. How freeing to give up the power. Not give it up totally, but share it. Warmth raced through her that had nothing to do with the sex and everything to do with the closeness and intimacy on all other levels.

"Couldn't you just do this forever?" she said, totally relaxed.

Sam rocked his hips from side to side. "It would be fun to try."

Her next orgasm caught her unawares, a huge, sweeping flood of release that ricocheted through her to him and took him with her.

"Wow!" She lay atop him, too spent to move.

"Yeah." She felt the satisfying weight of his arm around her, the deep, comforting rhythm of his breathing gradually returning to normal.

Eventually reality intruded, and she realized they had stopped.

She raised her head, seeing the gray haze of predawn outside the limo windows. "Where are we?"

"Mount Rush."

"Why?" She sat up and started to straighten her clothes. Sam did the same.

"Great view of the sunrise."

"Don't tell me you're a romantic at heart?" She made her words slightly scoffing, a sad attempt to convince herself that she wasn't impressed.

"Guilty as charged." Zipped and tucked back in, he sat up and reached for the champagne in the ice bucket. "I figure, what can be more impressive than a champagne sunrise?"

Actually, Sam himself was more impressive, but Kennedy kept the thought to herself. It was too scary to explore.

He opened the door of the limo and helped her out.

Kennedy caught her breath at the sight of the city sprawled far below them. If felt like they were on top of the world, a world newly discovering color as the sun slowly made its appearance in the distance. Color seeped across the horizon like liquid gold on fire, infused with a pink so deep it defied description. Sam draped his jacket across her shoulders, passed her a glass of champagne, and snugged her to his side, words unnecessary as together they witnessed the birth of a new day.

Kennedy leaned against him and drank in the sight, awash in total contentment in the moment. She pushed away all the internal warnings that told her the feeling wasn't real and couldn't possibly last.

Just because she had relinquished control and enjoyed the results once didn't mean she was about to make a habit of it.

Eventually Lisa grew tired of tossing and turning. She pulled on cropped workout pants and a top, scraped her hair into a ponytail, laced her sneakers, and let herself out of the villa just as the hint of dawn lightened the sky.

She took a deep, refreshing breath and set out at a good pace, using the silence and the forward motion to try and walk out her angst. It had worked in the past, a keep-herself-sane-and-in-balance safety valve. The air smelled different here on the east coast compared to the west. Different bird-song. A different energy altogether. And wasn't that why Kennedy had brought them here in the first place?

Yet she didn't really care about the sexcapades. She cared about her friends, and she didn't want to let them down. But most of all, she was tired of letting herself down.

Instead of thinking for herself, choosing for herself, she let everyone else dictate what she ought to do. Even on this trip, all events were orchestrated by Kennedy. And she knew Kennedy too well to believe there was anything coincidental with Ted's appearance. Once more, she'd let herself be manipulated. Well, no more!

Deep in thought, she hadn't realized where her steps were taking her till after she had cut through the golf course and arrived at the clubhouse. It was still far too early for anyone to be golfing. The clubhouse was locked up tight, but she recalled the night Richard had snuck her in there, showed her his trophies, and told her they didn't really mean anything.

"So what *does* anything mean? What's worth it?" She spoke aloud into the dawn stillness.

"You couldn't sleep either?"

She whirled at the familiar voice, wondering if she had imagined it.

Near the corner of the building stood Richard, looking very real and desirable.

"What are you doing sneaking up on me?"

"I showed up for work ridiculously early," Richard said. "What are you doing here?"

"I don't know," Lisa admitted. "I just started off for a walk. No particular destination in mind."

"You're a little early for a golf lesson," he said flatly.

"And I hope not too late to offer an apology for last night," Lisa said.

Richard was silent, offering no help.

"I didn't mean to be so . . . so . . . immature and juvenile last night," she finished finally. "I'm not sure what got into me, but I don't like it."

"Where's the poster boy?"

Lisa shrugged. "Who knows? Who cares?"

"You looked like you cared last night."

"I was an idiot last night. Please don't hold it against me."

He gave her a smile that made her heart leap up into her throat. "On one condition."

"What's that?"

"Come take a drive with me."

She clasped her hands together to keep them steady. "Only if it includes a stop for coffee."

"I'm sure that can be arranged."

Richard found a twenty-four-hour coffee shop, and Lisa clutched the warm cardboard cup as their vehicle jounced over an unmarked road that wound along the coastline, ending between two grass-dotted sand dunes. Directly across the water, cresting the horizon, the sun sprang into view.

"Can we get to the beach from here?"

Again she was treated to that heart-melting smile. "I'd say it's required."

Richard grabbed a blanket from the backseat and led the way. The path zigzagged through dune grasses whispering in the early morning breeze.

They reached the beach and Lisa sank ankle deep into the softest, whitest sand she had ever seen. Richard spread the blanket and she wasted no time removing her shoes and socks, digging her toes into sand that was already absorbing the sun's rays on top, but cool beneath the surface. She hugged her knees and leaned comfortably against Richard, sipping her coffee, suffused with utter contentment as she watched the sunrise.

"Humbling, isn't it?" Richard said.

Lisa blinked and turned to face him. How did he know her thoughts almost the same second she did? "It's a reminder of how insignificant we are in the overall scheme of things," she agreed.

"And how big our egos can be," Richard added.

"Did you have a big ego?"

"I didn't think so at the time. But it was easy to get a swelled head, given all the press and fan adulation. You start to think that all that attention is normal."

"And now you'll get a different sort of attention with your book."

"Which I plan to keep in perspective. What's next on your agenda, once you leave here?"

"I've got showings booked at the gallery. Artists depending on me to help build their careers."

"Sounds like a big responsibility."

"Originally it kind of fell into my lap, but I'm going back with a different outlook."

"What's that?"

"To make good things great. And work at making a difference to other people's lives along the way."

He traced her smile with one finger. "There's not even a shadow of the sad-looking woman I met almost a week ago."

She glanced away. "You look too deep."

"It scares you, doesn't it?"

"I'm not used to it. My upbringing hinged on surface appearances—keeping everything nice and pretty and unruffled at all costs."

"Life isn't like that."

"So I'm learning."

"But it's not all serious, either. Not if you don't let it be."

She turned so their lips could meet. "I think I need a reminder," she murmured just before his mouth closed over hers. She wrapped her arms around him and pulled him on top of her, relishing the feel of his hard length against her softer contours. She twined one leg around his, then rubbed her bare foot up and down his leg. Her breath caught and her nipples tightened pleasurably as she felt his response.

Behind him, the sun continued its upward climb, a nimbus haloing his silhouette.

He pushed her top up and out of the way, freed her breasts and cupped them in his palms, murmuring his approval as he traced their shape before paying homage with his mouth. He pushed them together and ran his lips across the eagerly waiting nipples, teasing the twin peaks. Lips closed, then open, then closed again, before he finally drew them into his mouth and suckled.

Lisa felt sensation ricochet through her to the juncture of her thighs where his erection pressed insistently, and she undulated her hips against him.

His hands continued to play with her breasts while his lips rediscovered hers in a kiss she felt all the way down to the tips of her toes.

His tongue blazed a trail from her lips, between her breasts, and over her ribs to her abdomen. As he slid down her length she lifted her hips to help him tug off her pants.

He dipped his tongue into her navel, then skimmed lower, through the thatch of curls to the hidden jewel of her clitoris. He blew lightly, encouraged her legs to part, needing Lisa to open herself for him in every possible way.

All of her was pulsing with need, engorged with blood, and when his tongue rimmed her feminine shape and his lips met hers, he felt the rush of her damp heat combined with his, building the pleasure to a crest until she exploded against him.

He continued to lick and lave, to taste her pleasure and allow it to fuel his own. Right now he wanted to make love to Lisa in a way no one ever had before, bathed in dawn's magnificence, the gentle lapping of the waves their only witness.

He nibbled the inside of each thigh, savoring the softness of her skin, then turned his attention to the back of her knees, the curve of her calves. He knelt and brushed sand from the instep of each foot and tasted her there as well, playing with one foot while grazing the other with his lips, nipping gently with his teeth. She lay writhing in impatience, her exposed femininity blushing deep pink, while farther in, beckoning him, he glimpsed rose red like the delicate inside of a seashell.

He tugged off his shirt and dropped it to the sand, then skinned off his pants. The sun was warm on his bare back, but not nearly as hot as the woman before him. He kissed and licked and nibbled his way up each leg to the apex, rewarded when her thrashing got more intense, as did the rise and fall of her breathing. He gently parted her treasures and honed in on the quivering jewel of her clitoris, feeling it swell beneath his tongue. Lightly, then with increased pressure, he tongued its plumpness, pulled it into his mouth, and heard

Lisa's strangled cry of release as her fingers dug into his shoulders.

Then she pulled him forward for a kiss.

"I need you now."

She spoke against his lips with an intensity that fueled his own need. In seconds, he'd rolled on a condom and made his way to paradise.

Chapter Fourteen

$\mathcal{L}$isa had never felt so free, so unfettered as she rose to meet Richard thrust for thrust, gloriously naked in the richness of nature's sunrise. Deeper, faster, harder, they fueled the flames of each other's passion. Awash in sensation, she felt ripples of pleasure rebuild from deep within, like waves cresting and breaking ashore, each more intense than the last until everything she knew, everything she felt, spun out of control, centered in the very simple here and now.

Riding her to those centrifugal heights, Richard swooped in for a kiss, then joined her, their bodies as in sync as their minds. Her orgasm stole her breath, trebled by the heightened intensity of him meeting her there, till gasping and spent, she released her grip and simply held him.

Gradually their breathing slowed to near normal and he rolled off of her, kissing her brow, her eyelids, her nose and her lips. Then he rose and pulled her to her feet.

"Come on."

"Where?"

"Where do you think?" He swept her into his arms and carried her to the water, wading in to chest height. She kicked her feet in abandon and tried to freeze-frame this moment in her memory. She'd need it on those gray, rainy days back in Seattle. And she felt a pang of sadness, aware she was already mentally preparing to leave, to rebuild the life she'd left behind.

In a happy way.

She'd suffered a loss, but she'd gained far more. She'd learned so much about herself and her responsibilities to herself.

Richard transferred her weight so she was wrapped around him, her legs clenching his torso, her arms clinging to his shoulders, rocked by the intensity of his gaze as it seared through her.

"So serious all of a sudden?"

"I guess it's part of who I am. Moving from 'here' to 'there' in my mind."

"'There' being Seattle?"

She nodded and nestled her head on his shoulder. "I don't want to go. I want to stay here—caught in the moment, no responsibility."

He spun her around. "Speaking of responsibility, I think I'm supposed to be at work."

She dimpled. "So I'm a bad influence?"

"The worst." He pressed a quick, hot kiss to her lips. "We're cursed, you and I. We honor our commitments."

"Ditto to that."

They used the blanket to towel each other dry before slipping back into their clothes. All too soon, they were back at the golf course.

Where reality intruded with a giant crash.

Lisa grabbed up the newspaper. "Oh, no!"

There they were, front and center. Kennedy, herself, Justine, and Ted.

The Hunt for Ted October! screamed the headline.

Lisa wanted to lower her head and crawl away. It was all there: the three Seattleites here to party, their sexcapades scavenger hunt culminating in the play for Ted October, their ideal man a one-dimensional calendar pinup. The story went on to claim the three had competed for him in an effort to see who would emerge the victor. The reporter made it sound like they had engaged in a laughable catfight over a man who didn't even exist. It seemed so sordid that Lisa felt physically ill as Richard skim-read over her shoulder.

"It's really not as bad as this makes it sound," Lisa said, glancing up at him. His expression was closed; impossible to read. "Say something," she implored as the silence streched.

"I already knew about it," he said, taking the newspaper

and putting it back. "I was hoping to hear about it from you, though. Not like this."

"How did you know?"

"Kennedy's the one you ought to be talking to, not me. Just how good a friend is she?"

"She's a best friend." But her words lacked conviction. Kennedy always seemed to have ulterior motives.

"You might step back and take a good, hard look at that friendship."

"What do you mean?"

"Where do you think the reporter got her information?"

Lisa paled. "Kennedy wouldn't do that."

"Your loyalty is commendable. I'm just not sure your friend deserves it."

Lisa turned on her heel and marched away.

The road outside the villa was bedlam. A TV news van was parked out front, alongside several cars sporting logos from newspapers and radio stations.

Lisa jogged past slowly, hardly able to believe her eyes, relieved when no one paid her any attention. She circled around through a neighboring villa and jumped the fence to the pool deck, going in the back way.

The kitchen smelled of cinnamon. Miles was at the sink mopping his face with a tea towel and wringing his hands. He started at the sight of her.

"There you are! We were worried sick when we couldn't find you this morning."

"I went for a walk. What the heck is going on?"

"I don't know exactly. They were lying in wait when Ted left."

"How did the paper find out about the sexcapades contest?" she asked.

Miles didn't meet her eyes. "I might have mentioned something to Ted last night."

"And he spilled?" Lisa felt a rush of relief. If Ted orchestrated this whole fiasco to cash in on the publicity, it let Kennedy off the hook. "Where is he now?"

"He said he had a meeting."

"I'll bet he does—with his publicist. Where are Kennedy and Justine?"

"I have no idea. Neither of them came home last night."

Lisa sank down onto a stool at the kitchen bar. "What a mess." Would Richard ever talk to her again? "Did you find out how Ted just happened to show up here so conveniently?"

Miles averted his eyes.

"Miles. Look at me. Ted's appearance was no coincidence, was it?"

"I'd like to know the answer to that, as well." Justine appeared in the kitchen doorway. "What's going on? I was practically assaulted on my way in." Justine looked disheveled and wrung out, last night's updo half undone and uncombed, her eyes dark in the paleness of her face.

"Did something happen with Eric?"

"You might say. His wife—excuse me, his ex-wife—went into labor and off he went." She gave a humorless laugh. "Seems it's my lot to always be the other woman."

"You're not the other woman."

"Thanks, doll. But apparently even when I'm *not* the other woman, I *am* the other woman. Miles, is there any coffee?"

"Give me a sec and I'll make lattes." Miles moved to the oven and pulled out a pan of freshly baked cinnamon buns.

"Did it not go well with Ted?" Lisa asked, more gently this time, aware that Miles's hand shook slightly as he eased the buns from the baking dish.

"As well as any one-night stand."

"Miles, I'm sorry." Lisa slid off her stool and gave him a sympathetic pat on the shoulder.

He shrugged. "I should be used to it by now. Why am I always attracted to the ones who are too good-looking for their own good?"

Justine laughed. "'Cause you're human, maybe?"

Lisa joined in, their shared laughter going a long way to ease earlier tension.

Miles flicked on the TV. "Might as well see what they're saying about us."

"Now that you've had your way with me, you're going to have to feed me," Kennedy warned Sam as they headed back to the waiting limo.

"Back to being bossy, are we?"

"Just letting you know what I need. That way you have no excuse for letting me down."

He tucked a strand of hair behind her ear. "I have no intention of letting you down."

Kennedy instinctively moved away. She might surrender sexual control for a lark, but daily life was a whole other matter.

Sam let her go, leaned forward to give the driver directions, then settled back next to her. "You know, you do a great job pretending to the world that you're bulletproof. I used to wear similar armor, back when I was younger and could handle the weight. Or so I thought."

"Armor? What are you talking about?"

"You know."

Choosing to let the topic drop, Kennedy leaned forward to stare out the window, feigning interest in the scenery as they made their way down the mountain and back toward town.

They were still on the outskirts when the limo followed a long, tree-lined driveway that led to an elegant mansion, far too large and impressive-looking to be a restaurant. The circular driveway looped in front.

Kennedy turned to Sam. "Where are we?"

"You said you were hungry. I have a standing date for Sunday breakfast with my mother."

Kennedy sank back against the luxurious leather. "I can't go in there. I'm in last night's gown, for heaven's sake. It's obvious neither of us has been home."

"I thought you were the original, take-me-as-you-find-me girl."

"Well, I am, but . . ."

The limo door opened. Sam gave her a gentle nudge. "Then there's no problem, right?"

She gave her trademark "who cares" shrug. "It's your mother, not mine."

Even as she said the words aloud, it seemed wrong to mention Sam's mother in the same breath with hers. Lillian was elegant and quality and a true lady. Mommy Dearest had been a piece of work, looking only to better herself and not caring who got hurt in the process.

Head high, Kennedy strolled into the retirement residence next to Sam. He was obviously a familiar figure, greeted by both residents and staff as they made their way to the elevator and from there down the hallway to the breakfast room.

The residence was modeled after an antebellum Southern mansion, gracious and well-proportioned. Breakfast was served in an airy, glass conservatory with lush greenery and the comforting murmur of a water garden.

Lillian was seated at a round, glass-topped table set with colorful floral-splashed linens, stirring a delicate bone china teacup. Kennedy was intrigued to note the table was set for three. Did Sam often bring a visitor on Sunday mornings? She instantly dismissed the thought as none of her business.

"Good morning, Mother." He bent down and kissed one porcelain-like cheek. "I've brought Kennedy along to join us."

"How nice," Lillian said with genuine warmth.

"Thank you for including me. What a beautiful room."

"It is most homey, isn't it?"

Not like any home *she'd* grown up in! Kennedy had just settled in to a glass of orange juice when Sam's phone rang and he rose.

"Excuse me, ladies. I really need to take this call."

"Don't worry, dear. Kennedy and I are more than capable of talking about you while you're gone."

He made a wry grimace. "Exactly what I'm afraid of."

Lillian watched his exit with genuine fondness, then returned her attention to Kennedy. "I count myself so lucky. He's my only child. And after the accident, for a while there I was afraid I'd lose him."

Kennedy ran her finger up the condensation on the outside of her juice glass, uncomfortable with the personal bent to their conversation. Did she really want to know things about Sam? There seemed no point when she was leaving soon. "I wasn't aware Sam had been involved in an accident."

Lillian sighed, her eyes clouded by memories. "Not to mention the difficulties after. The scarring, the teasing from the other children." She returned to the present. "But he's grown up to be a very handsome man."

"He certainly has," Kennedy agreed, her mind suddenly awhirl with a million questions.

"Are you enjoying your vacation here?"

"Very much. It's a lovely community."

"I was relieved when Sam decided to settle here. I was afraid that all our moving around when he was younger might have left him unable to stay put. But he seems content."

"So do you," Kennedy said. "Are other local retirement homes this nice?"

"Sadly, no. That's why benefits like last night are so important. I was left with a healthy sum after the accident, but many widows are less fortunate. Not that any amount can compensate for my loss, but I never had to worry about my financial future." She laughed. "I only worried about my son following in his father's footsteps to become a pilot."

Sam arrived to catch the gist of their conversation. "I thought you were joking that you'd be talking about me."

"Everything all right, dear?" Lillian asked.

"One of my clients changing his travel plans, that's all. I thought you approved of my career choice."

"I approved your right to choose," Lillian said drily. "There's quite a difference. Now if you would kindly turn that dreadful cell phone off, perhaps we could eat."

"The buffet's over this way," Sam told Kennedy. "Mother, I assume you would like your usual half a slice of French toast drowned in maple syrup, with one piece of crisp bacon?"

"Thank you, dear. That would be lovely."

Kennedy attacked the buffet like someone who hadn't eaten in days, mounding her plate with ham and bacon, fried potatoes, grilled tomatoes, and eggs Benedict.

"I love to see young people eat," Lillian said approvingly. "All this obsession young women seem to have with thinness is a dreadful waste of energy. Then you're my age and the appetite diminishes."

"I'm lucky to have a fast metabolism," Kennedy said.

"So what is it that you do back in Seattle?"

"I work for a large public relations firm."

"Public relations. Yes, I can see that you'd be very good at that."

"What makes you say that?" Kennedy asked curiously.

"I was watching you last night at the Gala. It was clear you were in your element."

"I seem to have a talent for people."

"Yes, and the newspaper did an amazing write-up on you and your friends. I was reading all about it before you got here. There's just one thing I wasn't clear on. What exactly is a sexcapades scavenger hunt?"

Lisa

Sexcapades

collect:

— your date's boxers
✓ his favorite golf glove
— a snip of his chest hair

score:

— a shooter he slurps from your belly button
— an extravagant piece of jewelry
— a picture of his penis

enjoy:

— sex in a limo
✓ water sex (indoors or out)
✓ sex outdoors (double points for daytime)
✓ skinny-dipping with your date
✓ dress-up sex
✓ him as your slave, bondage included
— *Give a blow job (because I never have)*

Chapter Fifteen

*K*ennedy left Sam with his mother and took the limo back to the villa, where she strode through the reporters with a terse "no comment." Normally she took every press opportunity that came her way and spun it to her advantage. She found her friends in the kitchen, stuffing their faces with cinnamon buns and lattes, laughing.

She paused to watch them before they noticed her, flooded with emotions that were foreign to her. She truly loved her girlfriends. Now the question was, did they love her?

"This looks cozy." She cruised in, in supercasual mode. "I thought you might be pissed."

"Why would we be pissed?" Lisa asked. Then she intercepted the look that Kennedy flashed at Miles. "Oh, because of the way you manipulated us. And invited Ted here."

"Kennedy invited Ted?" Justine asked.

"It seemed too good of an opportunity to pass up," Kennedy replied.

"Have you *seen* today's paper?" Lisa asked.

"What am I missing?" Justine asked around a mouthful of cinnamon bun.

Lisa leveled Kennedy with a look that made her almost squirm. "Why don't you tell the story, Kennedy? After all, it's yours to tell."

"Cinnamon bun?" Miles pushed the plate her way.

Kennedy shook her head. "I'm stuffed. I just came from breakfast with Sam and his mother."

"That sounds serious," Miles said, leaning his elbows on the bar.

"A serious disaster." Kennedy plopped onto a stool and buried her face in her hands. "And it's all my fault. My stupid idea to hunt Ted down through the modeling agency and have him show up here at the Gala and 'accidentally' run into us."

"But why?" Justine asked.

"Yes, we'd all like to know why," Lisa seconded.

"It seemed altruistic at the time. Lisa, you were sad. Justine, you needed to get that man out of your system once and for all. So here we are, away from home, playing hard to have a good time, and in waltzes our theoretical ideal man, thereby restoring everyone's belief that Mr. Right really does exist."

"You didn't think that was just a teensy bit contrived?" Lisa said.

"I didn't think of it like that," Kennedy said. "I thought it would be fun. A lark. Like the sexcapades."

"You didn't give us much credit for thinking or acting for ourselves," Justine said.

"But you were jazzed by Ted's appearance. I just wanted to give everyone hope, new possibilities for happy endings."

"Happy endings," Lisa echoed cynically. "Richard thinks I was using him for the sexcapades."

"Eric abandoned me for his pregnant wife's bedside while she gives birth."

"Ex-wife," Kennedy said, as if that made a difference.

"But it sounds like it all ended happily for you. You even told Sam about the sexcapades so he doesn't read about it in the paper. His mother, no doubt, loves you. The publicity will be good for your PR rep," Lisa said. "Though Ted broke Miles's heart."

"Yes," Justine said. "As usual, Kennedy finishes on top. You get the man. You won the sexcapades. You'll probably get a new job offer to boot."

"Hey!" Lisa piped up. "Who says Kennedy won the sexcapades?"

Three pairs of eyes zeroed in on Miles. "I haven't done the final tally yet," he said.

"Don't you think you should?"

"The day's not over yet."

Justine stood. "As far as I'm concerned, the contest is over. So is the friendship."

Silence flooded the room as she left.

Kennedy sent a stricken look Lisa's way. "She doesn't mean that."

"Sounds like she does," Lisa said. "She's pretty broken up about Eric leaving her the second his wife snapped her fingers."

"Ex-wife," Kennedy said, even though she knew no one was listening, "and she was giving birth."

"We love you, Kennedy. But you clearly have a lot to learn about girlfriends. Rule number one is no secrets. Rule number two is no manipulative moves."

"No one ever sent me that memo," Kennedy said.

Lisa shrugged and slid from her stool.

"Where are you going?"

Lisa turned and faced her friend. "As if I'd tell you and have you spill to the reporters."

"That's not fair, I—" But she was talking to air. Lisa was gone.

"I really screwed up, didn't I, Miles?"

"That would depend on what you hoped to gain. Deeper friendship with the girls? Major screwup. More of Kennedy being Kennedy, then I'd say you're right on track."

Kennedy fell into silent contemplation. She didn't even recognize herself anymore; not since she'd given over control to Sam. Her initial instinct was to try and fix things with the girls—but maybe this was her lesson. To ride it out, be patient, and see if things fixed themselves.

It was a huge risk. She didn't want to lose her friends, but bowing out was the only way she knew to prove to them that she had changed.

"Not that it matters, but the sexcapades were a three-way tie, weren't they?"

"By my calculations."

"Right answer," she said.

"It also happens to be the truth," Miles drawled. "You should try it sometime. Telling the whole truth, not just your version, or as much as suits you."

On that cheery note, he left her slumped over the bar and wondering what she could possibly do to make things right. Where Lisa and Justine were concerned she had to back off, hope and pray they still cared about her, warts and all. Wasn't that true friendship—accepting your friends' flaws? And if anyone knew her flaws, it was those two. In the meantime . . .

Leaping up, she went to her room to change her clothes, tidy her hair, and freshen her makeup, before she ventured out front to face the press.

"Kennedy, what's happening now? Where's Ted October? Who won the sexcapades?"

"We all won," Kennedy announced, head high, aware this was a time to be honest. "We had fun, and we met some great people. If anyone made mistakes along the way it was me, but boy, did I learn from those mistakes."

"Kennedy James admits to making mistakes?" echoed a cynical national reporter Kennedy had tangled with before. "Do tell."

"Friends deserve one another's honesty," she said simply. "You can have the best of intentions and still do the totally wrong thing, as I did. What I need to say right now is directed at Eric and Richard. If you're out there and hear about this, can you please contact us at the villa? There are some misunderstandings I need to clear up."

Kennedy heard the villa door opening behind her. Before she could turn her head, Lisa and Justine hauled her inside, then slammed the door.

"You really can't leave it alone, can you?" Justine hissed.

"I am! Really, I've changed," Kennedy protested.

Justine snorted.

"Since when do two wrongs make a right?" Lisa wailed. "Since when does airing dirty linen in public make things acceptable?"

"But I had good intentions," Kennedy said.

Both girls started to leave. Justine whirled and pointed a threatening finger. "Don't talk to those reporters again. Let it die."

"Where are you going?"

"Packing and getting the hell out of here. What do you think?"

Kennedy collapsed onto the floor. "I tried to leave it alone. Really, I thought I was."

"You're unbelievable."

"Why can't you both trust me to fix it?"

"Trust you?" Lisa said. "We don't even know you. Worse yet, I don't think *you* even know you."

Were they right? Was she so busy spinning sound bites, morphing into whatever she thought people expected of her, that she'd lost touch with herself?

The old Kennedy was no more, and the new one didn't

exist. Or did she? Her thoughts flew to Sam and his claim to know the real her.

Maybe it was time to trust him to give her the straight goods.

Through her musings she heard the noise crescendo out front. She went to the window, pulled aside the sheer, and peered out to see Ted holding court, clearly loving every minute. Would this make things better or worse? Would it take the heat off her and the girls or incite the furor? Did it even matter? She flicked on a local channel where live feed showed Ted on the villa doorstep.

Just as he finished, the doorbell rang.

"It's for you, Miles," she called, then headed upstairs to make herself scarce.

On the landing she met Lisa and Justine, suitcases in hand. All three stood eyeing one another warily. Kennedy swallowed. "How are you getting to the airport?"

"We called a cab," Lisa spoke.

Kennedy nodded. "Believe me, I never wanted things to turn out this way."

Lisa looked at Justine, then back at Kennedy. "If that was your attempt at an apology, it's as pathetic as you are."

Kennedy opened her mouth, then closed it. She'd never heard Lisa talk that way before. It was time she started thinking less about herself and more about others. She had to get over her fear of being vulnerable. What had Sam said? That she wasn't as bulletproof as she let on?

"Was that our cab at the door?" Justine asked.

Kennedy shook her head. "Ted. There might be one happy ending, after all."

They went to the railing and looked over. Directly below them, Miles and Ted were engaged in a heated exchange.

Lisa and Justine quietly put down their suitcases, and all three stood unashamedly listening as Ted pled his cause and Miles considered. When the two men embraced, all three girls broke into happy applause. Miles turned their way and gave them the thumbs-up.

Before they could savor the one bright spot in their day, the phone rang. "That'll be the cab." Justine and Lisa retrieved their luggage, paused on the main floor to say good-bye and good luck to Miles and Ted, then left without a backward glance at Kennedy.

Kennedy trailed downstairs. She heard the low murmur of Ted's and Miles's voices coming from the kitchen, peered out the front window, and heaved a big sigh to see the reporters melting away.

She knew what she needed to do next.

Kennedy was proud of herself when she managed to find her way to Sam's mother's residence without getting lost. She stopped at reception and got directions to Mrs. Watson's suite.

Lillian was seated at the window reading the paper, wearing a lavender silk robe. The sunlight spilling through the window created a halo around her carefully coifed silver hair and made her appear ethereal.

Kennedy paused in the doorway, suddenly reluctant to impose. Usually she was the first to blunder in where angels feared to tread. "Do it now and talk about it later" had always been her motto. It was the only way she knew to get things done. Maybe there was another way.

She took a breath and rapped lightly on the open door.

Lillian looked up and removed her reading glasses. Confusion clouded her features. Did she not remember her?

"It's Kennedy James, Mrs. Watson. I was here earlier with Sam."

"Yes?"

"I was hoping we could have some girl talk, just you and I." Never did she think she'd hear those words from her lips. Was this really her?

"Of course. Let me have them bring you some tea."

"Please don't bother." Kennedy entered the suite and took a seat across from the older woman. "I wanted to ask you about Sam. What happened to him when he was younger?"

"He doesn't talk about it," Lillian said. "I don't really blame him. It's so far in the past."

"You said something about an accident."

Lillian's blue eyes grew distant. "His father had a heart attack while flying. Sam believed, had he known how to fly, he could have saved him."

"They were in a *plane* when his father had the heart attack? My God, how awful!"

Lillian nodded. "Sam was a resourceful boy. He radioed for help, thinking the tower could talk him down with the plane, but they crashed and his father didn't survive."

"Was Sam badly hurt?"

"He was a mess. They put him back together as best they

could, but because of his age the plastic surgeon said he needed to wait till Sam's facial bones finished growing before they did the full reconstruction."

"How old was he when the accident happened?"

"He was twelve."

"The poor little guy."

Lillian nodded. "But they did a good job; he turned out very handsome. Like a movie star."

"Yes." Kennedy's heart ached for the scarred teenager. No wonder Sam was driven to be the best, confident, successful.

The fact that he knew all about being vulnerable explained how he could tap so closely into her deep, dark, hidden core of vulnerability.

She'd always thought she blamed her mother. In fact, she blamed herself: for not being good enough, not being worthy of her mother's love.

It was time to stop handing out blame. Time to accept the past and leave it there, the way Sam had.

In the back of the taxi with Lisa, Justine leaned forward and spoke to the driver. "I've changed my mind. Royale General Hospital, please."

Lisa reached over and punched her lightly on the arm. "Good for you! It's high time you snapped out of victim mode. You are no longer the other woman."

"I knew you'd understand." Her gaze softened. "You should do the same thing with Richard."

"I think so, too." Lisa sat forward. "Driver, Olympic View Golf Course, please."

"Which one first?" their driver grumbled. "The hospital or the golf?"

"Whichever one is closer."

The hospital was closer. Justine clambered out of the cab, then turned. "Oh, damn. My bags." She peeled off a handful of bills and passed them to the driver. "Driver, when you leave the golf course, take my bags back to the villa where you picked us up, please? I'll call Miles and let him know."

She hugged Lisa.

"Good luck," Lisa said.

"And you," Justine said.

Inside the hospital she spotted the information desk, where a man in military uniform stood speaking to the woman at the desk. When he asked for Anne's room, Justine realized this had to be Anne's husband. She backed away a few steps, then followed him into the elevator.

The taxi pulled up in front of the golf course. "Would you mind waiting a minute or two?" Lisa said.

"I guess I'm into it now," the driver said.

Lisa ran into the clubhouse. "Is Richard Davis here?" she asked the clerk at the desk.

"Rich? No, he left an hour ago. Personal stuff."

She dragged herself despondently back out to the cab, climbed into the backseat, and just sat there.

"Lady?" The driver turned around. "I don't have all day here."

"What? Oh. The airport, I suppose."

"You suppose?" The driver threw his hands in the air as if

pleading to the gods for help with passengers who had no idea where they were going.

That was the problem. She had no idea where she was going, or where she should be going. Heading back to Seattle held no appeal, but returning to the villa seemed to be only delaying the inevitable. For the first time ever, she didn't feel like going back to the city of her birth, but she was unable to shake the feeling she was leaving something important behind. Going back without whatever it was she came here to find.

The cab pulled up at the departure door of the terminal. Lisa paid and tipped the driver, reminded him to drop Justine's bags at the villa, then turned and went inside. She hoped she didn't have long to wait. An overtired toddler squalled loudly just ahead of her, ignored by the travel-weary parents. She put her suitcase down and pushed it along with her foot as the line crept slowly forward.

She took her eye off of it for a second to check her cell phone, and when she looked back, a hand was lifting her bag from the floor. "Need a hand?"

"Richard!"

He smiled down at her in a way that told her all was suddenly right with her world. "I was afraid I might have missed you."

"I stopped at the golf course," she said.

Her words stopped him cold. "You did?"

All she could do was nod.

"Why?"

"I didn't want to go home yet. Not before you and I . . ." She paused. "Spoke again."

"Do you have to go now?'

She shook her head. "I just didn't know what else to do."

"I have a great idea. Come on—my car's right out front."

Chapter Sixteen

$\mathcal{J}$ustine scurried to keep up with the soldier who strode along in front of her scanning room numbers. Abruptly he skidded to a stop and made a sharp right turn through a doorway. Justine slowed and kept walking. It's not as if she could follow him in and inquire about Anne's progress.

She reached the end of the hallway only to realize it was a dead end and she would have to turn around and walk past the room a second time. She had almost made it past when Eric emerged, masked and gowned. She glanced around, seeking escape, but Eric spotted her and ripped off his mask.

"Justine?" He gave her an amazed look.

"Hey, Eric." She tried for nonchalance. "How are things going in there?"

"Anne's husband just arrived. A lucky break for me."

Her heart plummeted. "Were you hating it that much?"

"Hating it? Not at all. But it's where the husband ought to be, not the ex-husband. What are you doing here?"

"Me? Oh, I . . ." No chance of making up a sick friend she was visiting. "I didn't want to leave the island without seeing you one last time."

"That's good. Because I had every intention of following you back to Seattle as soon as I could."

"You did? I mean, you would have?"

They stood gazing into each other's eyes, oblivious to the hospital bustle around them.

"Give me a couple of minutes to wish the new parents well," Eric said finally.

Justine could only nod. Just then from inside the room they both heard a weak cry like a newborn kitten.

"Sounds like the twins' father got here just in time," Justine said. "It's lucky you were there when Anne needed you."

Eric trailed a hand down the side of her face. "That was the hardest promise I ever kept, since I wanted to be with you."

"I love it that you didn't let her down."

She waited while he peeled out of his hospital garb and popped into Anne's room for a sec.

"Let's get out of here."

"Where to? The boat?"

"I've got someplace else in mind."

*   *   *

Kennedy felt as if she'd had an epiphany as she walked out of the senior care mansion far lighter than she walked in. The fact that she wanted to share her revelation was scary, but it was too late, anyway. Lisa and Justine were gone. Who else would know or care what this meant to her?

Sam!

She found him outside the mansion, leaning against the side of her rented Jag convertible. Her steps slowed when she caught sight of him, then speeded up again. She pulled out her well-rehearsed "who cares" swagger as she made her way to his side.

"Fancy meeting you here."

"I went by the villa. Miles filled me in on the girls' leaving. What were you talking to my mother about?"

She avoided his eyes. Suddenly, opening up to him felt too scary. "Just girl stuff."

He gripped her arm, forced her to look at him. "Something's changed. You're different."

God, he knew her so well! "In case you haven't noticed, I have a real talent for driving away people who care. Why haven't you bolted with everyone else?"

His eyes seared right through her to her core. "Surely you can do better than that."

She gave a humorless laugh. "I wish I could, but I can't. For some strange reason, I seem to have started to care about others."

"You always cared. You just didn't know how to show it.

You brought the girls here and lined up Ted's grand appearance because you care. And I'm guessing you came to see my mother because you care."

She nodded. "Lillian told me about the accident when you were young."

"And now you're going to treat me differently because of it?"

"How can I not, knowing what you must have gone through?"

"I'm still me, Kennedy. You went through tough stuff, and you're still you."

"I don't know *who* I am anymore and it terrifies me."

"You're admitting your fears."

"Along with my failures," she said. "I'm a terrible friend."

"You need to be a friend to yourself, first."

"I don't know how. It's something I never learned."

"And you need to forgive your mother."

"My mother's not like your mother. She's evil."

"Unless you move past that, it's always going to hold you back."

Kennedy opened the car door, got behind the wheel, and started the engine. "Good-bye, Sam. Thanks for the life lesson."

She drove away from him, wondering why she felt such a massive, wrenching loss. She started to shake and couldn't stop. She finally pulled over to the side of the road and sat there. When the sobs came it was as if a dam had broken open inside her, spilling out every last tear she'd held inside her all these years.

When the tears finally subsided, she felt spent but good. That's when her cell phone rang. It was Miles, and he sounded excited. "Kennedy, you need to call this number right away."

Richard drove the back roads with the ease of a man who knows exactly where he's going. Lisa exhaled a fluttery sigh, gazing at his profile, then at the way his hands held the wheel. She loved his hands. Strong and masculine, with elegantly tapered fingers and short-trimmed nails. Face it; she loved everything about the man.

"When do you think you'll be touring the Pacific Northwest promoting the book?"

"As soon as I can swing it." He slid her a sideways look that promised it would be sooner rather than later, and she felt butterflies bashing around in her stomach.

"Where are we?" she asked, more to offset her own nerves than real curiosity as Richard pulled the car to the side of the road and turned off the engine.

"From here, we walk."

"Walk where?"

"It's a wilderness garden made up of all native plants, some of which were bordering on extinction. I come here a lot. I find it peaceful."

The pathway he guided her along was bordered with wild clumps of grasses and plants. It meandered through the dappled shade and sun beneath a canopy of leaves springing out from gnarled tree branches.

Short, weathered pickets of wood that had once been a fence did their best to cordon off the area. As they moved closer to the heart of the garden, Lisa found herself caught up by the peaceful sense of past generations.

"I feel almost like it's welcoming us into this special sanctuary," she said in a hushed voice.

"Exactly. I'm glad I had a chance to share it with you."

Her heart warmed to his words, embracing the thought that they might have other special places and times to share.

Rounding a bend, they came upon a mystical-looking pond. Water plants dotted the surface, while reeds ringed its perimeter. A grassy knoll on the far side was the perfect spot to sit and savor. Richard led her there and spread out a blanket he had brought from his car.

She smiled at the memories it evoked, hoping she and Richard would make lots more memories together. "This is the blanket from the beach the other day, isn't it?"

He settled in beside her, his shoulder brushing hers. "I think everything I own has its special memories of times I spent with you."

"You've known me less than a week."

"It feels like forever. And I want it to be forever."

Lisa smiled as Richard reclined on the blanket, arms pillowed behind his head, staring up at the leaves overhead, backlit by a cloud-flecked blue sky. She propped herself on one elbow so she could enjoy watching him.

"Do you believe in destiny?" she asked.

"I believe something brought you into my life, whether you want to call it destiny or something else."

"I've done things I never thought I'd do in my life since I've known you."

"Nothing you regret, I hope."

"Not a single one. Except . . ."

"Except?"

She smoothed the palm of her hand across the plane of his chest. "Except not meeting you sooner." He captured her hand and raised it to his lips, kissing each fingertip before his tongue traced a pattern in the palm of her hand. Her body tingled and her heart reared up in happiness.

"Did you just write I love you in the palm of my hand?"

He grinned. "Call me a sentimental fool."

Lisa bit down hard on her lower lip and blinked back emotional tears.

"What?" he said.

"I've never been loved like this before, where I feel full to the bursting point."

"That's the great thing about love. There's always room for more."

She leaned over and brushed his lips with hers, softly at first, then with increased pressure. "I like the thought of much, much more. More everything."

"Do you think we'd travel well together?"

"I'm sure we would. What did you have in mind?"

"Once the book tour is behind me, I've got commitments abroad to design several golf courses. Maybe you could check out the local art scene."

"I bet that I could. Right now, though I'm far more interested in checking out the very local scene." She pushed up the hem of his shirt, revealing his hair-spangled abs and the softer hair ringing his navel. She unfastened his belt and giggled.

"You're such a good influence. I'd never made love outside before I met you, and now it's my new favorite thing." She nibbled across his middle and felt his muscles tighten as her tongue teased. Slowly she made her way to his navel, traced its shape, then let her tongue dart lower till it bumped the impatient tip of his erection, rising up to meet her.

"Mmm." She wet her lips and slowly slid them back and forth against the velvet tip, savoring his taste and his reaction. She slid down the zipper on his pants, allowing freer access.

She heard the hiss of his indrawn breath as she parted her lips and took just the tip of him inside her mouth. Lips sheathing her teeth, she continued to torture him, taking in no more than half an inch at a time.

"*Lisa.*"

Awash in the feeling of her own power, she proceeded to explore his length with her mouth, moving her lips from root to tip with a light sucking motion, over the top and down the other side, never taking him fully inside her mouth.

"You know how to torture a guy."

She smiled in satisfaction just before she lashed him with her tongue and took as much of him inside her mouth as she could. His groan of pleasure echoed through the quiet.

At one point he tried to pull free. "Lisa, I can't, I'm going to come."

"Isn't that the idea?"

She stroked him as she sucked, felt him shudder in release, his hands tightening in her hair, then releasing as he eased her face up for his kiss. She smiled into his eyes. "I've never given anyone a blow job before. How'd I do?"

He pulled her close. "I think I've created a monster."

She felt him begin to stir against her. "I hope so. We're far from finished here."

Kennedy was still sitting behind the wheel of her parked car when Sam drove up and parked behind her. He got out of the car, and she did as well. They stood on the side of the road in the middle of nowhere, their eyes meeting warily.

Sam touched the tear tracks on her cheeks. "Bad news?"

She shook her head, at a total loss for words.

"Anything you care to share?" He shoved his hands in his jeans pockets.

She cleared her throat. "I didn't think you'd be interested in sharing. Not after I dug into your past when I had no right to."

"I would have told you eventually," Sam said. "It's no big secret."

Kennedy's mind tripped on the word "eventually." "I figured it was a part of your past you'd rather forget about."

"Stuff like that plays a huge role in shaping who we are today. I'm not about to pretend it didn't happen."

"You mean, if the accident hadn't happened, you'd still be you, only you'd be different."

"Exactly. Same for you. Maybe one day you'll trust me enough to tell me what it was like."

Her heart stumbled at the subtle reference to the fact that they would be in each other's lives past tomorrow.

"That's twice you've done that now."

"Done what?"

"Implied that this isn't going to end when I leave here."

Sam smiled down at her in that slow, melty way of his. "Did you just finally figure that out?"

"Actually, it was about twenty minutes ago," she said.

"What happened twenty minutes ago?"

"I returned a phone call from a PR firm here, and they offered me a job."

"What did you tell them?"

"That I had to think about it. It's a great job offer, but I had to see how you felt about it. This island is too small for me to be here if you hate me."

"I don't hate you, Kennedy. And I think you'll discover this island is just about the perfect size."

Chapter Seventeen

"If not the boat, then where are we going?" Justine asked Eric.

"Someplace we can be alone with no interruptions."

That place turned out to be Eric's villa on the golf course.

"It's gorgeous," Justine said. Beautiful like the glossy pages of a decorating magazine; it revealed nothing about the man she had fallen for.

"It used to be the show home when they first started selling the properties," Eric said. "I just rent it. I didn't feel like buying anything other than my boat."

"So this isn't your art, or your taste? Thank goodness."

"You're a decorator," Eric said. "What's wrong with it?"

"I prefer a place that speaks to the personality of the owner. This feels too staged."

"So if I buy a place, will you help me create a place that suits me?"

"Of course I would." Her heart plummeted. He wanted to *hire* her? "Why did you bring me here, Eric?"

"I'm an old-fashioned guy. It occurred to me that we've never made love in a real bed."

Justine shrugged. "So let's go."

"What's your rush?" he teased. "Got a plane to catch?"

"As a matter of fact, yes."

"Not till tomorrow, though, right?"

"Does that mean you want me to spend the night with you?"

"The day, the night and many, many more."

He reached for her and she stepped away. "I'm afraid that would never work."

"Why not? Don't tell me you don't have feelings for me. I know it's happened fast, but—"

"I do have feelings for you," Justine said. "But I also want to have a family one day. And I know that's not what you want."

"Why do you say that?"

"Because the kid issue is what broke you and Anne up."

"It wasn't having or not having kids. It was Anne's total obsession around the issue."

"I might get a little obsessed myself. It's not a passing whim; it's something I feel very strongly about."

He pulled her close and nuzzled the top of her head with

his chin. "What will it take to convince you I'm there with you, every step of the way?"

She sighed against him and then pulled back. "A person doesn't change how they feel all of a sudden, Eric."

He tugged her back, tilting her head up till her gaze met his. "I was Anne's labor coach until her husband showed up, and though I don't for one second wish she and I were still together, I realized that I could take on that role for real. To be there for the birth of the child I create with the woman I love. The woman I want to be with forever."

Justine melted against him. "Which way to the bedroom?"

He ushered her in and turned on the bedside lamp. She noticed the bed was already turned down.

"Were you expecting company?" she teased.

"My housekeeper is eternally optimistic. I'm surprised there's not a chocolate and a red rose laying on the pillow."

Justine framed his face in her hands and pulled him down for a kiss.

He pulled back. "Why are your eyes shiny with tears?"

Justine blinked the moisture away as she smiled. "Because I've never been this happy. And I have the feeling you and I are going to make the most amazing child someday. In fact, I think we ought to start practicing right now."

"I'm with you on that."

She felt the tenderness with which he slowly removed her clothing, making her feel more beautiful than she had ever felt before in her life.

She slid beneath the covers. "Now it's your turn."

He wasn't nearly so slow stripping off his pants and shirt

before he slid in next to her. She turned to him and skin met skin in a crescendo of tingling nerve endings as she twined her limbs around his.

Their first kiss was almost tentative, as if they were kissing for the first time, even though it felt as if their bodies had known each other always.

He stroked her from upper thigh to rib cage, the rugged warmth of his palm leaving a trail of fire in its passing. She shifted restlessly, inhaling his own unique fragrance, the essence that was him far more stirring than any manufactured cologne.

She moaned deep in the back of her throat as he kissed her lips, eyelids, cheekbones, chin, and more, leaving no inch of her untouched.

She longed to worship and explore him as freely as he did with her, but felt incapable of doing anything besides lying there and enjoying him. Besides, they had many more opportunities ahead, days and nights to be together. The thought made her shiver in anticipation.

She felt the weight of his erection pressing against her leg as he inserted his knee between her thighs, urging them apart. She reached up and raked her nails lightly across his chest, lingering on the flat male nipples, hearing his breath catch as she teased them the way he teased hers.

He ducked his head and captured her nipples between his lips, one at a time. She felt them harden in response, radiating sensation like sun-warmed honey through her chest and arms and torso, to settle lower.

She sighed in pleasure. "That feels so good."

She felt the weight of his hand stroking her stomach from hip bone to hip bone. "I can't wait to see you grow heavy with our child."

His hand slid lower and sleeked through the curls guarding the entrance to further female delights.

She rose up against his hand, sharing the moisture of her desire. Her breathing deepened as he honed in on the sweet spot and fondled it gently, sending her to new heights of desire, before skittering away, leaving her panting and breathless for more.

"No fair," she said.

"All's fair." He stretched out atop her, his rugged body finding and fitting all the soft contours of hers. She wound her hands around his neck and kissed him long and hard in longing and surrender.

His pelvis rocked hers and she slid her legs apart, inviting him, enticing him. His lips abandoned hers to forge a pathway between her breasts, past her torso, to hone in on the petal-like softness of her treasure trove.

She moaned softly as he made contact, his tongue and lips fighting the most divine duel for mastery. She twined her fingers through his hair and allowed the waves of pleasure to lap over her, through her, consume her until, with a sob of surrender, she rode the final pleasure pinnacle of release.

Her body still quivered in the aftermath as he positioned himself for possession, kneeling between her legs with a look that sent a surge of emotion rioting through her. Justine thrilled at the possessive way he took her. He slid into her with a divine friction that had her rearing up to meet him, her hands clutching his shoulders, her legs wrapping around his torso. And together they found their own magic place to celebrate their triumph and completion.

"Follow me," Sam told Kennedy, and for once she didn't ask where. Happy to relinquish control, she kept his taillights in sight all the way to the airport, where she parked next to him and got out.

"Are we going someplace?" she asked.

"What do you need to do to wrap things up in Seattle?"

"Not much. Give notice to my employer. Pack up my apartment."

"Then let's go." He led the way into the hangar where his plane landed.

"You mean, fly to Seattle right now? Isn't that a little impulsive?"

"Would you have me any other way?"

She grinned. "No. But I need to fix things with the girls before I do anything else. I only hope it's not too late."

"We could beat them back," Sam said. "You could be at the airport when they land."

"You'd do that for me?"

"Sweetheart, I'd do pretty much anything for you. Let me make a few calls."

Sam wasn't gone long. "I have news, all of which sounds good. First, the girls are still on Walker Hook. Justine is with Eric at his place, and Lisa is with Richard. Second, what do you think about hiring me to fly you all home together tomorrow?"

"I don't know. Can I afford you?"

"I'm certain we can work something out."

"Sounds great. Then what shall we do tonight?"

"Well . . . I've never had the chance to test out the bed in my plane."

Kennedy grinned. "So what are we waiting for?" She raced up the plane's steps and inside. "Sure you don't want to do it in the cockpit?"

"Too cramped," Sam said.

"It's not much smaller than the limo," she pointed out.

"Nothing cramps your style, does it?"

Falling in love might, Kennedy thought. She fought down the wave of panic, unsure if she could do this. Could she leave her job, move across the country, and tie her life to this man? All of a sudden she felt dizzy. She saw spots before her eyes, and her breath came in shallow gasps.

Sam pushed her into a seat and forced her head down between her knees. "Breathe slowly. Slow and deep. In and out. Breathe with me."

The warmth of his hand on the back of her neck soothed and relaxed her, and the dizzy spell slowly passed.

"Sorry about that," she said, straightening. "I don't know what happened."

"You were hyperventilating. In panic mode."

She tossed her head back. "I wasn't panicked."

"You were like a wild animal in a leghold trap, contemplating gnawing off a limb to free yourself," Sam said.

Kennedy felt her defenses crumble as she melted against him. "Damn you."

He cupped her face in his hands. "I'll never tie you down, Kennedy. I'll never hold you back. I'll always only love you."

"You don't think that love is a tie?"

He caught her hand in his, and linked their fingers. "I think two is always better than one. Two energies. Two brains. Two lives intertwined."

She leaned in for his kiss. "Teach me," she said against his lips.

He kissed her gently with reassurance in his kiss, then picked her up and carried her to the bed.

He laid her down as if she was the most precious thing in the universe. She gazed up at him. It wasn't in her to be passive, but here she was, waiting for his move.

He laughed softly as he tugged off her shoes. "One thing I *do* know is that our time together will never be dull, and you will never be predictable."

Her heart leaped. He *wouldn't* clip her wings. He'd encourage her to soar, to find her way with him by her side, cheering her on. She rolled over and attacked the buttons on his shirt, burying her nose against the familiar smell of his skin, a smell she would never grow tired of. She straddled him, pinning his hands above his head.

"Damn you, I love you."

"I know," he said smugly. "And we're going to have a helluva lot of fun."

He rolled over, taking her with him, laughter alternating with kisses till they were both undressed.

When he caught her hands above her head, she didn't feel trapped, but worshipped as he rubbed his body along hers.

Kennedy sighed at the feel of skin on skin. Her body burned and tingled needfully and she undulated against him, translating her needs.

"Patience, my lovely."

His mouth was against her neck, tonguing the sensitive cord at the side, gliding down to where shoulder meets neck.

She trapped one of his legs between hers and swiveled her hips, creating a divine friction against his hardness. He slowly dragged his fingertips from hers, down the sensitive inner skin of her arms, to graze her underarm and her breasts, shimmying down her length, kissing and nipping and loving every inch of her till she thought she might explode.

"I *need* you, Sam."

"For always," he prompted.

"Always is a long time," she said.

"And always is what we'll have."

She shuddered as his cock sought the moist essence of her womanhood. The tip grazed her clitoris and she sucked in her breath, a ripple of prelude starting to build. She moved her hips invitingly, imagining everything they would create together.

And when he finally entered her, the world whirled in Technicolor, a kaleidoscope of shapes and tastes and sensations beyond anything she'd ever dared to imagine.

Kennedy

Sexcapades

collect:

- ✓ your date's boxers
- ✓ his favorite golf glove
- ✓ a snip of his chest hair

score:

- ✓ a shooter he slurps from your belly button
- ✓ an extravagant piece of jewelry
- ✓ a picture of his penis

enjoy:

- ✓ sex in a limo
- ✓ water sex (indoors or out)
- ✓ sex outdoors (double points for daytime)
- ✓ skinny-dipping with your date
- ✓ dress-up sex   —*bustier counts!*
- ✓ him as your slave, bondage included
- — *1/2 point—I was the one tied up!*
- — *Meet his mother*

Chapter Eighteen

$\mathcal{J}$ustine and Lisa met up at the check-in counter at the tiny Walker Hook Airport and exchanged blissful, happy glances, then burst into giggles.

"Ready to go?" Justine asked.

Lisa gave a satisfied sigh. "What a night. You?"

"I have to admit it felt pretty strange to wake up next to a man in bed with me this morning. That'll take some getting used to. In a good way," she added.

"So there will be other nights, other mornings?" Lisa said.

"Oh yeah," Justine said. "And we're starting on a baby right away."

"Really!" They checked their luggage, picked up their boarding passes, and headed for Security.

"Being a labor coach gave Eric a whole new outlook on fatherhood," Justine said. "When are you seeing Richard again?"

"Very soon. He's kicking off his book tour in the Pacific Northwest."

"That's great, Lise. He's such a good guy."

"I know."

"It's weird without Kennedy here," Justine said. "She ought to at least know how fantastic things turned out."

"Despite her meddling," Lisa said.

After going through Security, they found their gate and settled into the lounge to wait.

"Knowing her, she's giving this some time to blow over," Justine said.

"You mean rather than show up like nothing happened?"

Lisa was flipping the pages of her magazine and Justine was staring out the window when they both heard the announcement over the public-address system.

"Passengers Justine Bates and Lisa Green, please report to desk number nineteen. Passengers Justine Bates and Lisa Green, please see the attendant at desk number nineteen."

"Please don't tell me our flight has been delayed," Justine grumbled.

Together they approached the desk.

"Sorry for any inconvenience," the woman said. "May I please see your boarding passes and identification."

Lisa and Justine dug out their boarding passes and passports and handed them to the woman. "What's this all about?" Justine asked.

"Thank you." The woman returned their paperwork. "Your departure gate has been changed. You need to go back toward Security, look for gate twenty-two A, and identify yourselves to the person behind the desk there."

Lisa sighed as they collected their hand luggage, then made their way to gate 22A.

"We're Green and Bates," Lisa said. "We were told our departure gate had been changed."

"Very good. If you could follow me, please? You've been upgraded."

"Sweet," Justine said. "I love flying business class."

"I just want to get home," Lisa said. "The sooner I get there, the sooner Richard arrives in Seattle on his book tour. What about Eric?"

"He's talking about relocating," Justine said with a happy smile. "And luckily there is no shortage of golf courses in the Seattle area."

As they followed the attendant outside and across the tarmac, Justine took a deep breath. "Say good-bye to the deep South."

"Yes, I'll miss the lush tropical air."

The attendant stopped and ushered them toward a set of steps leading up to a private jet. Lisa stopped short and Justine did the same.

"This can't be our flight," Lisa said.

"There must be some mistake," Justine agreed.

"Please step inside," said the agent. "The pilot will explain everything."

Lisa and Justine exchanged looks, and started up the stairs. "Might as well get to the bottom of this," Justine said, just as the pilot appeared in the doorway.

"Ladies, welcome aboard."

"Sam. What's going on?" Lisa asked.

"Oh, I know," Justine said. "Kennedy's up to her usual tricks."

"You can blame this one solely on me," Sam said. "I have to go to Seattle, and figured you'd be much more comfortable here."

"This is a serious upgrade," Justine said as they entered the plane's cabin. The table was set with fresh flowers, champagne, tropical fruit, croissants, cheeses, and juice. Jazz was playing on the sound system, and the comfy leather club chairs were laid out with blankets and pillows.

"I could get used to this," Justine said.

"Me, too," Lisa said. "But it doesn't feel quite right without Kennedy here. Sam, do you know where she is?"

"She's in the terminal, waiting for me to phone her if you two agree to see her. If not, you still travel back in style."

"Oh, lord." Lisa dropped into a seat and helped herself to a frozen grape. "Neither of us can hold a grudge longer than a sneeze. Tell her to get her skinny ass in here now."

Sam smiled. "I was hoping that's what you'd say."

Moments later, Kennedy came flying across the tarmac and up the steps. She burst into the cabin and hugged Lisa and Justine at the same time.

"I'm a terrible, terrible friend, and I don't deserve you

two. I am so going to miss you when I move." She was bab-
bling, making little sense.

"Moving? What are you talking about, moving?" Justine
asked.

"I've been offered a job here at Walker Hook."

"Doing what?" Lisa asked.

"PR—what else? Some executive took a liking to me dur-
ing the Ted fiasco and offered me a job. Can you believe that?
And Sam needs his apartment redecorated, so Justine, will
you come back and do that for him? I'm not living in that
museum."

Sam just shook his head. "What have I let myself in for?"

"Sweetheart, you haven't seen anything yet. Can you
please go fly this plane so I can spend some time with my
girlfriends?"

"Just don't think you can always boss me around." He
grinned.

Kennedy gave him a long, soulful kiss. "We'll take turns
being the boss."

"Dare I believe what we're seeing and hearing?" Justine
asked Lisa. "Our friend, Kennedy, the original find 'em, fuck
'em, forget 'em gal, is finally settling down?"

"Hey, when it's right, it's right." Kennedy opened the
chilled bottle of champagne and poured them each a glass.
"Now I want to hear all the details about *your* men. Oh, but
wait. Miles gave me this package and said we're to open it
once we're in the air."

"What's in it?"

"No idea."

The girls ripped open the package and hooted with laughter as they thumbed through the contents. It was all the things they'd collected for the sexcapades.

Justine picked up a plastic ziplocked bag, then dropped it with a shudder.

"Whose chest hair is that?" Kennedy asked

"Who cares?" Justine snagged Eric's boxers. "I guess I should return these one day."

"Is that a naked picture of what I think it is?" Lisa leaned over and picked up a rather graphic photo.

Kennedy laughed and snatched it away. "There are some things that are not meant to be shared. Not even among the best of friends."